Dedicated to Paul Spragg.
He loved Doctor Who *so much*,
Doctor Who *loved him back.*

Thanks to Ani Murr
for advice about guilt.

And to Ailsa Sladen.
For being.

BBC DOCTOR WHO

The
Blood Cell

BBC

DOCTOR WHO

The
Blood Cell

James Goss

B\D\W\Y
Broadway Books
New York

Copyright © 2014 by James Goss

All rights reserved.
Published in the United States by Broadway Books, an imprint of
the Crown Publishing Group, a division of Random House LLC,
a Penguin Random House Company, New York.
www.crownpublishing.com

Broadway Books and its logo, B\D\W\Y, are
trademarks of Random House LLC.

This edition published by arrangement with
BBC Books, an imprint of Ebury Publishing,
a division of the Random House Group Ltd.

Doctor Who is a BBC Wales production for BBC One.
Executive producers: Steven Moffat and Caroline Skinner.

BBC, DOCTOR WHO, and TARDIS (word marks, logos, and devices)
are trademarks of the British Broadcasting Corporation and are used
under license.

Library of Congress Cataloging-in-Publication Data is available upon request

ISBN 978-0-8041-4092-8
eBook ISBN 978-0-8041-4093-5

Printed in the United States of America

Editorial director: Albert DePetrillo
Series consultant: Justin Richards
Project editor: Steve Tribe
Cover design: Lee Binding © Woodlands Books Ltd 2014
Production: Alex Goddard

10 9 8 7 6 5 4 3 2 1

First U.S. Edition

I

'Do you know who I am?' I said.

One thing you learn. It isn't what prisoners say that tells you most about their guilt. It is their silences.

The man said nothing.

'Do you know who I am?' I repeated.

The man glared at me rudely across the desk. 'I know who you think you are,' he growled.

I pushed the tray of his possessions towards him. The various trinkets rolled and rattled and glistened brightly among the scraps of newspaper. I could see his eyes follow them like a cat's.

'These are yours?' I said to him. He nodded. I could see how badly he wanted to hold them. People are like that with objects. Personally, I've never really cared for that kind of thing, but people cram their pockets and their lives with memories of no value to anyone other than themselves. I had nothing like that. Not now.

I nodded to Bentley, and she walked across my

office smartly. I handed her the tray.

'These are Prisoner 428's personal effects,' I informed her. She inclined her stiff neck curtly. Bentley possesses two attributes – stiffness and sourness. Like a lemon meringue. The absurd image amused me and I smiled despite myself. Try as I might, I never can quite get on with Guardian Bentley. Whatever I do – it's never quite good enough for her. But she has her uses. And I knew that she would like me to be strict. I was here to show Prisoner 428 that I meant business.

I indicated that she should take the proffered tray. 'I have taken possession of Prisoner 428's personal possessions,' she told me formally, making no effort to find another word to provide any variation in the sentence. Bentley was like that. Her speech was as dry as the manual, and just as correct. Her uniform, her shoes, her haircut. Everything about her was frostily neat.

'Very good, Bentley,' I nodded to her. 'See that they have an accident on the way back to storage, will you?'

Prisoner 428 was on his feet, yelling that I didn't understand or something. That was a mistake. At the first sign of protest, a Custodian swept forward from the wall, its claws clamping into his shoulders. To give him his due, Prisoner 428 didn't cry out, he just winced, turning on the robot with fury. 'Let me go,' he snarled.

That cut no dice with the Custodian. The things were built without even a semblance of a face, just a solid cylindrical body and various sharp appendages. People got tired of shouting at them because there was nothing to shout at. Most lacked voice processors, so they could not answer back. They were completely cold metal and even when they were hurting you did so without giving off the slightest response. My first girlfriend had been exactly like that. Once, long ago.

Prisoner 428 was struggling loudly against the Custodian, which was stupid. The more you did that, the tighter the Approved Safe Restraining Hold became. 428 must have been in a fair amount of pain, but he just looked angry, his manacled hands waving away the pain like it was a buzzing fly.

'Those things are important, man, just look at them,' he said, making direct eye contact with me. Which was remarkable. No one here looks me in the eye. Even Bentley (who is allowed to) avoids it.

'I have examined them,' I informed Prisoner 428, allowing just a trace of tiredness to leak into my tone. 'You have nothing of any value. Baubles, gadgets and scraps of paper.'

I picked up one object from the tray Bentley held, a tiny pen-like thing and tapped it against my teeth, smiling back at Prisoner 428, enjoying the eye contact. He had a face made for fury and was making the most of it.

'Paper? You've clearly not looked at any of it!' snarled Prisoner 428. 'Get this thing off me, stop being an idiot and let's have a nice chat, shall we?'

Bentley blinked. I think even the Custodian winced. No one talks to me like that.

Sensing the awkward silence, Prisoner 428 glanced around. 'What?' he snapped.

'You would like me to read these documents?' I asked him, reaching towards the tray that Bentley extended.

'Yes,' snapped 428. 'I don't suffer fools gladly. Pick up a piece of paper, read it, and save us all a lot of time.'

The moment held. I picked up a scrap of newsprint. It had a headline about troubles on HomeWorld. I dangled it neatly between my finger and thumb and then let it fall back. With a smile.

'You will address me as 'sir',' I informed him hotly. I was surprised at how angry I sounded.

His stare didn't waver. His face may have been made up of storms, but his eyes were a wonderfully clear blue. His rudeness was almost refreshing. Because I'm so important, no one is ever quite themselves around me. But Prisoner 428 was clearly out to be different and I was prepared to enjoy it. For a while.

'Stop being an idiot, *sir*,' he replied, flashing me a rather lovely smile. 'Just read the thing, and then we can all go home.'

I snapped my fingers and the Custodian released

him and retreated, gliding back into its alcove. Prisoner 428 tried rubbing his shoulders, but his manacles wouldn't allow him, so he settled for pummelling his shoulders with his fists.

'You know,' 428 considered, 'as a massage, that was rather bracing. Come up with a good name for it, and you could clean up in health clubs. Mind you, you don't even really have to bother with a good name. I mean, take Zumba.'

After this puzzling remark, he shook himself down like a wet dog and then settled back into his chair, throwing one chained leg over the other and stretching. Then he pulled his face into an expression of contrite humility.

'See what I'm doing? I'm making an effort to make a good impression on you, sir,' he said almost sweetly.

'It's a little late for that,' I replied.

'Oh, I know,' Prisoner 428 nodded. 'But honestly, I really do always give people every effort. No one ever just listens to me. Which is a shame. I dunno about you, but I've always fancied knocking off early for a quiet night in with *Call the Midwife*. Do you get that here, sir?'

'No,' I told him. For some reason a smile was stuck on my face and it was taking an effort to shift it.

'Pity,' he sighed. 'It's a lovely show about babies and bicycles. I like both these things. If only real life was that easy, eh?'

I coughed.

'… sir,' he added dutifully, then looked up, almost puppy hopeful. 'See? We're getting on better, aren't we, sir? I don't suppose I could prevail upon you for my valuables back, could I? As valuables go, they really are valuable.' A pause. 'Sir.'

With a smile, I shook my head.

'Last chance,' he said, 'Look at my papers. You'll understand.'

I hesitated.

428 gave me an encouraging nod.

Then I clicked my fingers.

Bentley opened an incinerator hatch with casual ceremony and slid the contents of the tray rattling into it. Prisoner 428 looked as though he was going to protest, and then watched them go with rapt silence. 'Well, that's a pity. That would have saved a lot of time.'

There was a waft of heat as Bentley closed the incinerator hatch and turned back to me. 'I regret to inform you, sir, that the personal effects of Prisoner 428 were lost in transit.'

'Remiss, Bentley, most remiss,' I tutted.

She nodded, seemingly taking the reproof seriously, and then, with a rigid bow, departed. I may not like Bentley, she may not like me, but I do think we are both very efficient in our own way. Bentley's way is more rigid. Everything about her reminds one of this fact. Constantly. Bentley gets things done.

By contrast, Prisoner 428 was slouched in the metal chair, wriggling himself comfortable.

'Now then, Prisoner 428, where were we?' I leaned back in my chair, making the most of its padded luxury. Prisoner 428's chair was, needless to say, a sheet of metal bolted to the floor.

'You were asking, sir…' 428's tone was a little dead. Did I detect the first signs of defeat? 'You were asking if I knew who you were, and I was merely raising a valid query about the nature of identity. It's a sliding scale,' he shrugged. 'I should know. Sir.'

'I shall repeat the question, Prisoner 428. Do you know who I am?'

Prisoner 428 had done surly, angry, rude, and chummy. Now he yawned. 'Yes, sir. What you want to hear is that this is a prison on an asteroid in deep space. You're the Governor of it.'

'Very good, 428,' I said encouragingly. 'Not a prison. We call it *The* Prison. And only the very worst criminals are sent here. I'm reliably informed that you're the worst of the lot—'

'Well, I'm innocent,' flashed 428 with fury.

'You all are, I know,' I tutted. 'Please do not interrupt me again, or I'll have the Custodian sever something. I was going to say that I am informed that you are the very worst criminal in the sector, guilty of heinous crimes against the HomeWorld government. But,' and I made myself appear as casual as 428 was, 'let me tell you something – I'm not interested in the details of your crimes. That's all in the past. While you're here, you're under my care. I view all of the prisoners here as my friends. And I'd like to include you on that list. Can I, 428?' I leaned forward just a little. And smiled.

428 considered the offer. 'I'm not in the habit of calling my friends "sir".'

'Make an exception, there's a good fellow,' I told him. 'You're in a lot of trouble 428 and—'

'Oh, can we stop all that?' snapped Prisoner 428. 'My name's the Doctor.'

'It sounds like a criminal alias. And names are not allowed here.'

'Well, tell you what, since we're friends, let's both make exceptions, shall we?'

Sometimes you have to bend Protocol in order to achieve a positive outcome. I was glad that Bentley wasn't here to see this. She really wouldn't have approved.

'Very well then, Doctor,' I said with my warmest smile. 'Do you know why I had you brought here?'

428 considered. 'Was it about the escaping?'

'Correct! Very good, 428, it was about the escaping. You're a new arrival. You have a lot to learn. You can't escape from The Prison. Even if you continue to get out of your cell, there are the Custodians, Bentley's guardians, the walls, the fences, the external defences to get through and then, finally, a very long walk home through deep space. In case you've missed it from the view as you arrived, we're on an asteroid at the edge of the system. We get few supply ships. There's honestly no way out, and yet you keep on trying.'

'Oh, I do,' 428 nodded warmly. 'Call it a vocation.'

'Some inmates weave baskets. They find it very calming.'

'I've never had much time for wicker,' muttered 428. 'I'll just carry on escaping, if it's all the same to you.'

'Of course it is. Be my guest.' I waved the idea away magnanimously, reached across and patted him on the shoulder. I noticed with pleasure that he winced slightly. Clearly it was a little sore. 'Escape as much as you want, my friend. I'm fully confident in my team's abilities, but I'm sure they appreciate the practice. And, thanks to you, they have had a lot of practice of late.'

'I do try my best,' Prisoner 428 said smugly.

I toyed with the idea of cramming him down the incinerator, but beamed instead. 'Well then, everyone must have a hobby, I suppose.' I stood, indicating he was dismissed. 'Off you trot, 428, back to your cell, and enjoy your escapades.'

'You don't understand,' the Doctor – 428 – didn't move.

'I beg your pardon?'

'You don't understand, sir,' Prisoner 428 repeated. 'I did all the escaping for one purpose only. So that I could meet you.'

'Did you now?' I paused. I gave 428 another silence to tell me more about him. 'You wanted to meet me?' I leaned forward, interested.

'Yes,' he said.

'Well, I'm pleased to have unlocked that particular achievement for you.' I nodded, satisfied. 'Perhaps you could learn a language next?' I beamed, and motioned to the Custodians. 'Take him back to his cell.'

'No, you idiot… sir.' The Doctor was on his feet, leaning across the desk, eyeball to eyeball with me, yelling fiercely as the Custodian sliced from the wall and wrapped electrified tendrils around him. 'I had to meet you!' he cried furiously, ignoring the pain, 'Because I had to warn you. You have no idea what's really going on here, do you? Unless you listen to me, a lot of people are going to die.'

2

I make it a rule not to look into the pasts of my prisoners. We all have skeletons in our closets, don't we? and I try my best to be a man of my word. When I said to Prisoner 428 that I wanted to be his friend and that the details of his crimes did not concern me, I meant it.

All the same, he had been behaving extraordinarily. New arrivals often do. The Prison is an unusual place and takes some getting used to. I remember when I caught my first glimpse of it from the shuttle and my spirits, already low, slid down into my boots and then hid beneath my socks. I knew what The Prison was going to look like – in my old job, I'd been involved in the earliest planning stages, after all. But, when all of the worlds in our system, even now, are so colourful, to have helped create something so utterly grey and cold was horrid. The twinkling anti-gravity belts and external defence grid cast little lights on the darkness, creating pockets of almost-colour where you could trick yourself into thinking that the grey became a rich purple or even was tinged with shades of blue.

But really, the asteroid was just a formidable fist of rock, huge and forbidding and dark and so very final. We'd taken an unwanted lump and we'd put the most unwanted people in the sector in it. And forgotten all about them.

As my shuttle got closer and closer on that first approach, I found myself caught up in schoolboy imaginings, trying to think of a way of escaping. What would I do if I was a prisoner here? How would I get out of my cell? How would I get off the asteroid? I couldn't help myself, I just got wrapped up in my enthusiasms. But, as the rock drew closer and closer, those childish dreams died in me, and I don't think I've ever been quite the same since.

Honestly, most of the many security defence systems are pointless. There's no way off this prison. Shuttles don't even land, instead a one-way transport crosses the Defence Array and beams supplies and prisoners directly into the reception area. I'm not saying that people haven't tried to get out, but it never ends well. The only way to escape from here is to die. Eventually, everyone realises this fact. And after that, I have no further trouble with them.

But what about Prisoner 428, who would prefer to be known as The Doctor? Well, what of him? I'd seen his type before, so many times. He'd tirade and shout, organise a furtive protest group, then a more blatant one. There'd be tiresome acts of rebellion, overt campaigning, perhaps a samizdat newsletter, maybe a few mass escape attempts. Inevitably, there'd be injuries (on his side), and his support would mutely drift away until Prisoner 428 stood alone, even sadder than when he first arrived.

I wanted to spare him that. Of course I did. It was my humane duty to do so. He was my friend, whether he wanted to be or not. So that was why I was breaching my promise to myself and finding out a little more about him. For no other reason than his own good, of course.

I blipped Bentley and she arrived, as stiff and immaculate as ever.

'That was a bit of fun just now, wasn't it, Bentley?' I said.

'If you say so, Governor.' Bentley's tone was cold, but the edges of her mouth twitched. She always teased me with the promise of a smile. I'd only ever seen her actually smile once, and that was when an escape attempt had gone horrifically wrong. Poor Marianne. To be truthful, I'm glad I'd never seen Bentley smile again.

'Will you take tea with me?'

Bentley inclined her head in assent. 'If you so order.'

'It's hardly an order. Simply a custom between friends.' We were not friends. It was stupid to pretend so. And yet, I could not help trying. She worked for me, and yet she treated me little better than her charges. No matter what I did, no matter how correct, stern and thorough I was, she always surveyed me as though there was jam on my uniform. I don't even know why I was offering her tea. The whole thing was a stupid idea. But I'd made the offer, so I should press ahead with it. I beamed at her, a little forced, perhaps. Still – a drink between colleagues. A Custodian brought us tea and we both pretended to enjoy it. The drink was all right, so long as you didn't question where the tea came from. Or the water.

Bentley settled in the metal chair opposite me. She was the only person who never seemed put out by its iron discomfort. She was waiting for me to speak.

'I think we'll have trouble with this "Doctor", don't you?'

She nodded. 'Are you going to call 428 by his name?'

I was expansive. 'We can afford to be generous. I doubt he'll be with us for long.'

For a moment, Bentley almost caught my eye. 'Would you like me to arrange…?'

'No, no!' I assured her hurriedly. 'I simply mean that we've seen his type before. It never ends well, does it?'

Bentley considered the airy statement seriously. 'We still have 112 on Level 6.'

It took me a moment to remember the number. 'Oh.' She meant Marianne Globus. Poor Marianne.

Poor 112. A dear friend. 'Ah, yes.' Neither of us said anything for a moment. 'How remarkable of you to remember, Bentley. I'd quite forgotten, really. I've almost completely forgotten all about her. Well, what's left of her.' I was pretending to be airy. In reality, the very thought of what had become of poor 112 made me feel ill. 'And how is she?'

Bentley almost faltered for a moment. 'I have not supervised her personally for some time. But the Custodians on Level 6 have not reported anything negative about 112's condition or her pain management.'

Poor Marianne. We'd stopped thinking about her. Level 6 was pretty empty. She'd not even seen a human guardian for quite some time. Oh dear. 'I should probably arrange a personal visit with her at some point.' I didn't fancy it at all.

'Indeed.' Bentley inclined her head, pleased I wasn't rebuking her.

'Don't worry about it,' I assured her. 'You do a splendid job overseeing the running of the entire prison. You can't worry about every little thing. That's my job. My wife used to tell me a saying from Old New Earth: "Take care of the pennies, and the pounds will take care of themselves."'

Bentley inclined her chin, interested. 'What does that mean, Governor?'

'I'm not entirely sure. Then again, she also used

to tell me: "Don't sweat the small stuff." That's the problem with archaic prayers. To our ears, they seem so contradictory and elusive.'

'A little like Prisoner 428?' It was, for Bentley, a joke.

'Yes,' I beamed, keen to show I was pleased with what Bentley had said, as it fitted with where I wanted the conversation to go. 'Sounds a lot like the Doctor! Remarkable fellow. Yes.' I leaned back, feeling all thirty-six supporting comfopockets of the chair do their luxurious work. 'You know, I'm rather keen we don't end up with another Prisoner 112 situation on our hands... Well, all over our hands.'

'What would you like me to do?' Bentley waited for me to speak.

'I was wondering if, in this case, forewarned is forearmed. I was thinking I'd have perhaps the tiniest of glances at 428's records. Do you think that would be wise?'

'Whatever you think best, Governor.' Bentley kept her tone neutral. 'It can be arranged. I can call his files up over the TransNet. It may take a little time.'

Communications were appallingly slow here. The relay of TransNet satellites back to the System HomeWorld were erratic. In the early days there had been an idea that we could use the TransNet for near-live relays of entertainment programming, news and communications back with loved ones. Sadly, once The Prison had been set up we had discovered that the TransNet supplier had done a woeful job of the relay. Even the simplest communications were painfully slow. Prisoners just arrived here, often without us knowing who they were. Entertainment was sent in from the shuttles on old-fashioned hard copy (whoever said the data crystal was dead?), and what little news we received was either via extremely brief text bulletin or summaries burnt to hardcopy. In the beginning it had felt ever so isolating, but now we'd grown used to it. Almost to enjoy it. Prisoners and Guardians. We were all hermits together.

Sensing she was dismissed, Bentley made to get up, her cup of tea half-finished. I waved her to remain seated. 'It's all right,' I assured her. 'I can do it from my terminal.' Sometimes I think she assumes I'm a hopeless old has-been, but I tapped the computer to wake it up. It responded sluggishly. The terminals they've fitted us with were supplied by the same contractor who put in the lamentable TransNet system. They're awful. The icons swam slowly into view. I tapped the one for 'Records'. And then tapped it again. And then finally accepted that the thing had frozen.

Back home I'd been used to asking my tablet everything, constantly. Now I bothered with it barely once a day. I was forced to rely on my own wits. I was rather proud of that. The freedom it gave me. All the same, it would be nice if the systems worked just once.

Bentley was standing, heading for the door. 'Perhaps it would be best if I looked up the records for you,' she offered gently.

She really does think I'm past it. Ah well. There was another cup of tea in the pot, so I poured it. I'd not finished it when Bentley came back in with 428's records hardcopied up into a folder. I settled down to read them thoroughly over the rest of the tea. After a few pages I stopped reading thoroughly and merely glanced, and then I pushed the folder aside, sickened.

I picked up the cup, but the tea in it had gone cold. I couldn't face that either.

I realised Bentley was still in the room, watching me, curiously appraising my reaction. In many ways, she's like one of the Custodians, silent and solid and grim. I'd never tell her this, of course. She has feelings, I'm sure she does. Somewhere. She'd feel terribly hurt.

'You've read about the Doctor's crimes?' she asked.

'Prisoner 428,' I said firmly. He no longer deserved a name. Sickened, I pushed the folder over to her with distaste. 'Take this away.'

My tablet had rebooted and I used it to login to 428's cell-cam. His was as spartan as all of our prisoner accommodation. Each box contained a shelf for sitting and sleeping. And a door. There were no windows because there was no view. Only Guardians were allowed to see the stars and space. Prisoners simply got to see the walls and each other. Each cell was a regulation size, although those on Level 6 were perhaps a trifle smaller. And yet 428's cell seemed cramped, as though the man filled the room.

He paced the area, tugging away at the orange uniform, as though trying to pull it into something other than the shapeless garment it was. The orange was the only colour that the prisoners saw, and, as it was everywhere, they no longer noticed it.

I stared at him in fascination. So this was the man, the man who had… I shook my head. His crimes hardly bore thinking about. I hated him. It was unprofessional of me to do so, but I hated him.

I wondered when 428 would grow tired of pacing. They all did eventually. When I was a child, we still had zoos. My prisoners were the same as zoo animals, treading out the limits of their confinement, as if somehow they could wear away the floor and the bars, before they finally accepted defeat.

Prisoner 428 had not yet given in. Had not yet realised that he would never leave The Prison.

I zoomed in on his face, trying to read his crimes on it. We were about the same age, but his features looked stretched under the effort of containing his guilt, as though trying to keep several lifetimes of tiredness and anger at bay. It was a face that was commanding. Not exactly handsome, but certainly unforgettable. It chilled me to think that that was the very last thing so many of his victims had seen. Not a sunset, not the faces of loved ones smiling a sad goodbye, but just that angry face boiling away like a dying star. I shuddered.

Whatever it takes, I vowed to myself, I will make you pay for what you have done.

The alarms roused me. I'd wandered away into my thoughts, which was always a mistake. There's so much to do on The Prison, and it doesn't do for a Governor to daydream. Even when things are running smoothly.

I glanced back at the cell-cam and started. It was almost as though 428 was staring through the lens, right at me. Those eyes. The terrible things they'd seen.

Hastily I cut the feed. And then the alarms blarted.

On The Prison we have a lot of alarms. None of them are good news and all of them sound like lost souls shrieking. This wasn't the particular agony of the 'Prisoner Escape' alarm, but it was still fairly shrill. We'd been hearing it a lot recently.

Bentley knocked abruptly on my office door and then entered. 'Systems Failure,' she announced in capital letters. We both knew this already, but Prison Procedure stated that the Governor had to be informed. I nodded, and stood.

We both walked swiftly through to the Control Station, where Custodians slid silently between terminals. Screens showed every cell, every corridor, every area of The Prison. A giant map of the whole asteroid glowed. In theory it should be showing where the systems failure was, but instead it was partially obscured by an icon that read 'UPDATING… UPDATING…' Most unhelpful.

The Prison diagnostic system had been put in by a separate contractor to the one who had provided the tablets and the TransNet. By all accounts they hadn't got on well with each other, and had done an equally shoddy job.

I looked at Bentley moving swiftly between the Custodians and accessing verbal updates from her fellow human Guardians. If only everything in life could be as efficient as Bentley, I thought. Perhaps a little warmer. Just a shade. But she was everything you could hope for in a crisis.

The truth was there was very little we could do. These systems outages were growing increasingly regular and there was no explanation. If this latest one proved true to form, they'd pass in anything between three and five minutes and then it would be business as usual. But while the alarms sounded, it was up to Bentley and her team to ensure that no core systems were affected. She'd tasked some Custodians to try and work out the root cause, but so far they'd reported nothing. Instead, they'd become expert at riding these emergencies, reallocating resources on the fly to ensure the locks did not fail, the containment grid was maintained and the environment system stabilised. This sometimes meant the evening meal was undercooked, the gravity a little light or the air slightly stale. So far we'd not had to make any huge sacrifices.

Late one evening, Bentley and I had sketched out some Emergency Protocols. Or rather, I'd made some suggestions, and she'd listened and then said 'If I may…' and corrected them all. But we were prepared. Just in case it got worse and the power drains couldn't be switched easily around. It hadn't been an easy conversation. We'd agreed that we'd have to enact them if the systems failure reached seven minutes. That would be the end. A blinking red clock timed how long the current outage had been.

The Prison Map glowed 'UPDATING… UPDATING…' and the clock read that four minutes had passed. Bentley continued moving with quiet efficiency. Custodians continued to slide antenna across panels, reporting on further failures and the smaller successes of reallocating resources.

The clock passed five minutes. I noticed the human Guardians looking at each other nervously. An element of panic was creeping in. Most of the time, we can forget that we are on a rock in deep space artificially made to contain life. When the systems work, then we put the fragility of our existence from our minds. But suddenly it springs back up during an alert, and we remember that, if the power fails completely, that's it. We've a limited supply of oxygen. Even if we called for help, even if that help set off from the HomeWorld or the nearest colony immediately, then there's very little chance of it reaching us before the air runs out. We're all of us, prisoners and guards, already buried in our tomb.

The clock passed five minutes and fifteen seconds. A horrid first. I wondered if I should say something calming or encouraging, or do something that smacked of lunatic normality, such as making myself a cup of tea. I wouldn't drink it. It would just be there for show. Your Governor is not panicking. He is drinking tea. He is calm. So you can be too.

The clock reached five minutes and twenty-nine seconds. A new and rather formidable record. I could see Bentley looking at me, trying to get my attention. But I stared ahead. We had ninety-one seconds before we had to start making terrible choices. Let's enjoy the ninety-one seconds as best as we could. If we survived, the decisions we took would be on our conscience forever.

At five minutes and forty-one seconds, the Prison Map suddenly cleared. 'SYSTEMS NORMAL,' it reported. The alarm stopped. The red went out of the light.

Suddenly it was awfully quiet, apart from a collective breath of relief and a slight sweaty tang of panic to the air.

'Well done, Bentley,' I said. 'Well handled.' As if she had somehow averted a terrible crisis. The truth, the terrible, frightening truth, was we had no idea what was going on.

My comm blipped. It was a call from Level 7. Reluctantly, I took it, knowing it would be the Oracle.

The Oracle's fat face filled the screen, jowls wobbling as he shook his head from side to side.

'Oh dear,' he purred. 'That was a close one, wasn't it?'

One of the few things that Bentley and I could agree on was a hatred of the Oracle. Everything about him irritated. Considering neither of us had any physical contact with him, he was still somehow repellent. His hands were everywhere. They always filled the screen, playing an invisible keyboard whenever he spoke, fluttering, rising and falling.

The Oracle liked to do only two things in life – to predict the future and to say 'I told you so'. His predictions very rarely seemed to actually come true, but then again, they were always so nebulous in nature that he could claim anything after the event.

He did so on this occasion. 'Didn't I tell you there'd

be purple vibrations ahead?' he said, throwing his fingers up above his hair and then letting them drift down to his chin. 'Well… I would call a nearly six-minute system failure decidedly purple. Wouldn't you?'

He pursed his lips and waited for a response. The annoying thing about the Oracle was that we needed him. Without him, there'd be no one to take care of Level 7.

The Oracle gave up waiting for a reply and leaned back, building his fingers into a steeple and then a cathedral, 'I shall tell you this one thing, my friends, there are solid purple times ahead. You mark my words.' He cut the terminal.

I went back into my room, to calm down, to relax, to mull, to try and plot out the future, to try and think of something. My tablet had reset to the view of Prisoner 428's cell. He was stood there, staring out at me again, impassive. One eyebrow was raised, curiously. As though he was waiting for something. Could he be behind it all, I thought, shuddering.

I switched off the tablet, the ghost of that stare remaining on the screen for a moment. What did he know, I thought? What did Prisoner 428 really know?

3

The girl. Visitors to the Prison are rare, but we do get them from time to time. They hire private shuttles – occasionally from the HomeWorld, more often from one of the more dismal colonies, and they fly all the way out to us. There's a landing pad. We never use it ourselves. The pad was specifically designed to be isolated from the rest of the prison. We knew the visitors would come.

Sometimes a whole family will turn up. A mother and father, a husband, some children. Sometimes they'll stand on the landing pad crying. Sometimes they'll stand there silently. Waiting.

There are no regulations for dealing with visitors. The Protocols merely state that, regrettably, prisoners are not allowed visitors. As a courtesy, the first time they come, I will always go out to the fence that separates the Landing Pad from the rest of the prison. The fence is little more than a symbol of the seventy-three systems that cannot be breached between the

Landing Pad and the Prison. Like everything else, if I so choose, under ordinary measures I can deactivate seven of those systems, to allow them to pass me objects. Such as, say, a petition. Usually it's a petition. Letters and presents for prisoners aren't allowed. Also, I cannot give the visitors anything. Even I can't access all seventy-three systems. Even I can't let someone innocent pass from inside the Prison to outside.

As I said, the first time someone visits, I will always go out to them. It seems humane. Sometimes they'll stand there clamouring and shouting through the fence. Sometimes there are placards. Sometimes just one of them will step forward and quietly speak to me.

'Do you know who I am?' I will ask them. They always do.

'We would like to speak to <insert name of prisoner here>,' that's how the best of them will go. I will politely reply that, sadly, that isn't possible.

'But we were promised TransNet communications with them,' they will insist. 'We have not heard from them since their arrival. We simply wish to know that <insert name of prisoner> is well. We love them. That is all.'

I will nod gravely and then reply: 'I can assure you that <insert name of prisoner> is absolutely fine and receiving approved treatment. The TransNet network is not currently operating at sufficient bandwidth to allow communications between prisoners and those on the HomeWorld. I can assure you that the problem is not at our end. I would recommend you raise this with the HomeWorld authorities. I am told that the current difficulties are caused by solar wind.'

They always look at me in an odd way when I say that. But it's what Bentley has told me, and I have to trust her.

They'll then ask if they can pass me letters for their loved ones. I will apologise and explain that communication over TransNet is all that is allowed for. I'll tell them I'm trapped by Protocols. They'll look at me in a funny way again. And then ask to pass me a petition full of hope and indecipherable signatures.

I've never understood petitions. People you've never heard of want you to do something. There's nothing I can do about it. I look after the prisoners, in accordance with my own conscience and the Protocols. By all means, send your petitions to the Homeworld Government. Perhaps they'll surprise us all by releasing someone, or just order me to accord someone extra privileges. But they never do.

I explain to the visitors patiently, and, I hope, kindly, that if you hand me a petition, I will simply scan it and send it by appallingly slow TransNet relay back to the Government. The uplink they have on their shuttle is undoubtedly much faster. But they insist I take it. Perhaps it makes them feel better, as though the long, expensive journey has been worthwhile. If so, then it's the least I can do to take it, and to look at them seriously and gravely. They never quite look back at me.

That's how a good interaction goes. Sometimes they even thank me for my time before they go away. I've had training to deal with the less ideal scenarios. Sometimes they scream at me. 'How could you? How can you live with yourself?' they shout. But then, those are questions no one can answer. We do what we do and we can live with ourselves. Somehow. That's the only answer anyone can ever give.

Anyway, that's a broad summary of how a typical first visit goes. The one where I have the courtesy to greet them.

The other times they come I generally leave them out there. Procedures say I only have to meet them once.

They stand there. They wave their placards. They peer hopefully through the fence. No one comes out to them. And, eventually, they go away.

They rarely visit a third time.

The girl, though. The girl would be different.

She arrives without any fanfare, she's just standing there on the launch pad. Curiously, the Defence Array hasn't picked up any approaching shuttle. We've not even properly had time to turn on the landing lights.

But that's all right, because she doesn't appear to need help landing her shuttle. She's just arrived, like a spell was cast.

She's also not properly dressed. Not a spacesuit, not even a flightsuit. Just an old-fashioned jumper and a neat, quaint skirt on her small, determined frame. She's even wearing a band in her hair. I remember people like her. It's been a long time since I've seen a Vintager. I thought they'd died out with Old New Earth. She reminds me curiously of Prisoner 428. The same sense that she's here, but that she doesn't belong.

Of course, I can guess she's come to see 428.

In accordance with Protocol, I went out dutifully onto the landing pad. She was waiting for me. She wasn't holding up a placard or a lot of tiresome pieces of earnest petition. She was just sat on a lump of rock, reading an actual paper book. When I reached the fence, she affected not to notice for a bit, just carried on reading, her nose wrinkled slightly as she turned a page. Then she folded down the page (on a priceless artefact! I hated her just a little), slid it into a pocket, and looked up at me with a smile. 'Sorry,' she said. 'Just got to a good bit. So… Hello.' She smiled, politely. 'How can I help you?'

'I'm the Governor here,' I said, already a little discomposed. 'It's more how I can help you, isn't it?'

'Well, if you say so,' she shrugged. Her patient smile made her face even prettier.

'You are with 428, aren't you? The Doctor?'

She nodded.

'Would you like to see him?'

She nodded again.

'Well, I'm afraid that's not possible.'

'Ah,' she looked serious, her hand thumbing the book in her pocket. 'I have come such a long way. And it would really be a good idea if you could let me see him.' And there we were. Back on familiar ground.

'Are you a relative. His daughter, perhaps?'

She laughed at that, a full-on, throaty, horrified laugh. 'Never tell him you just said that. He'd kill you.'

I frowned. She mentioned 428 killing, but almost casually. As though she was unaware of the full horror of what he had done. Or was wilfully ignoring it. I tried not to let it get to me. 'Are you, then, perhaps his… wife?'

She frowned then, her face clearly doing 'Oh, come on'. Sadly, I knew the type. 'My dear, I am sorry for you. You're unfortunately not the first to turn up here in your predicament. Perhaps you saw the Doctor's face on the TransCasts, or read about his trial, and you fell in love with him.' I ignored the squeaking protesting noises she made. 'You're here because you're infatuated with him, and you believe that, if you only met him, you could reform him. I know what you're here to do.' I shook my head sadly. 'You're here to save him from himself.'

The girl considered this. 'Well, right now, I do think he's a bit of an idiot. Does that count?'

Once more I was puzzled. She wasn't behaving like a lovelorn fan. She stuck out a hand, the fingertips not quite brushing against the fence, just crackling against Protection System #3, the electric field. She didn't snatch them back. She didn't flinch.

'Let's start again,' she said. 'Hello, I'm Clara. I'm a friend of the Doctor's. What brings you out here?'

'I'm the Governor,' I said, bowing in formal greeting. 'I am mandated to greet any person on their first visit to the prison in accordance with Protocol.'

'Just their first visit?' Clara raised an eyebrow.

I nodded. There had been some talk about my having to come out to all visits, but after a while it just seemed to emphasise the futility of the exercise. Bentley had assured me I didn't have to. I was grateful for this unusual kindness to me. 'I'm obliged to come out and talk with you once. After that, well, you're welcome to return as many times as you wish. But this is your one chance to talk directly to the Governor.'

Clara's frown deepened. 'Right then. So, for shorthand purposes, you're not going to release the Doctor, even though I've worn my smartest skirt?'

I shook my head.

'And there's absolutely no chance of a quick chat

with him?'

I shook my head again.

'Fine, then,' Clara shrugged. 'So it's just you and me?' She didn't seem that annoyed. 'Fair enough, although I do feel like the girl who found the lamp that granted her three wishes. Or something. You know how it is. For my next wish I would like infinite wishes.' She smiled.

I smiled back, despite myself. 'I am afraid I don't know the fables of your tribe.'

'Oh, don't you?' Clara's smile widened. There was something about this girl that was rather winning. She wasn't exactly treating this as a joke; more she was treating me as a human being. It had been, I suddenly realised, a long time since anyone had. Normally visitors just shouted at me. They never seemed to realise that I am as bound by the law as my charges, those I consider my friends.

She paced backwards and forwards across the landing pad for a little and then put up her hand. I guessed she was used to talking to people. Something in her manner – an educator. That was it. They did tend to be cranks and fanatics, although to describe this Clara as one seemed a little unfair.

'To summarise, the only thing you can do is listen to me, and you only have to do that the first time I visit?'

'That is correct,'

'But you do have to listen,' she grinned, as though struck by a thought.

'Of course.' It did seem the least I could do for the friends of my friends.

'Fine. Then I've got a fable for you,' she said, wagging a little finger at me. 'It's about a woman who was, ah, let's say a kind of Queen of Jordan. And this Jordan was determined to get exactly what she wanted in life. And so she married lots of kings. And no matter how many kings she married, no one gave her exactly what she wanted. One was an, um, singer. Of sorts. One was a warrior. One ran away back home in confusion. And one looked very nice in a thong. I think there were other temporary kings, but those were the main ones. Anyway, the point is that none of these kings gave the Queen of Jordan exactly what she wanted, but she kept on marrying them as she was determined to get what she wanted. She wasn't going to settle for anything less than perfection, and she was going to keep going, even if she ran out of kings. Which seemed likely.'

I considered this parable closely. 'And you're saying that you're like Jordan, Queen of Jordan?'

Clara nodded, biting her upper lip with determination. 'In so many ways you can't even imagine,' she vowed. She leaned close to the fence, the electricity sparking around her face. It flashed and flared in her eyes, and she looked grimly serious.

'Listen to me, Governor. I'm going to keep on coming back until you do what I say. Release the Doctor. Or a lot of people will die.' And then she smiled that sweet little smile, and just walked away.

Fanatics.

4

After the girl's visit, I stepped up security. I ordered a DoubleR watch on the cell of 428. I also asked Bentley to check and see if there could be any outside influence causing the power fluctuations. As the Defence Array showed no signs of Clara's arrival, perhaps she was somehow in hiding on the surface of the asteroid. The scanner sweep was negative.

The only thing that happened was that we had two more systems failures. Neither went up as far as five minutes and forty-two seconds, but still, they were serious enough that I ordered Bentley to send an error report back to HomeWorld. In case there was anything they could advise. Apparently the only immediate response from HomeWorld was a flurry of accusations and counter-accusations among the various contractors and subcontractors responsible for the building of The Prison. And the outages continued, although they were not as severe.

'Well, I suppose it keeps us on our toes,' I said to

Bentley. If I was hoping to get a smile out her, I was mistaken. No matter what I said, I could never get on the right side of her.

The Oracle blipped up from Level 7. He was peering through his fingers at me. He looked drunk. He often was.

'Oh, Governor, there you are,' his voice oozed delight.

'What can I do for you, Oracle?' I never enjoyed talking to him.

'It's more what I can do for you. The girl interests me.'

'What girl?'

'The one who came to visit. I could see it all through my mind's eye.' More likely through your tap into the camera relay. 'She seems delightful. I see a…' He took a deep sniff of the air. '… a vermillion path for her.'

A stubby finger prodded the camera, fingerprints squidging against the screen, 'I tell you now, she and I are going to meet quite soon.' He nodded at the wisdom of his own remark and then threw his hands up to mime fireworks in the air. 'And we shall light up the sky! So many vibrancies! See if we don't.'

I shook my head a little. 'I'm not sure you're her type.'

'No matter.' The Oracle, a shade disappointed, winked at me. 'I predict interesting colours for her and for… ah yes, Prisoner 428. That one casts a long, puce shadow over the future.'

I next encountered Prisoner 428 on the viewing deck. Unless you stand on the landing pad, it's the only bit of The Prison that offers a view of the stars.

It was late at night, and I was out there alone. I often came to the viewing deck on my own, to remember the past. I always came there without a Custodian, and I felt a momentary panic when I saw 428 standing there. I clicked my fingers and a Custodian emerged from the walls, gliding up to me, hovering and ticking as it awaited instructions.

'Prisoner 428!' I called. 'Explain yourself. What are you doing here?'

'Looking at the stars.' 428 didn't turn.

'For a start, prisoners are not allowed to look at the stars.'

'Seems rather cruel,' said 428. He still hadn't turned.

'It is done for your own benefit. Psychocriminologists adjudged that the sight would merely decrease prisoner morale.'

'That so?' 428 turned to me. His face was framed by the stars spinning slowly behind us, and for a moment I thought how oddly right that looked. 'Your psychocriminologists sound a pretty idiotic bunch.'

I couldn't disagree with him, so I moved on to point 2. 'Point 2. Prisoners are not allowed in this area of

The Prison.'

'Ah,' 428 clucked. 'Well, I'll make a note of that and avoid it in future.'

'Point 3. Prisoners are asleep at this time.'

'Tsk. I don't really sleep.'

'Point 4. Prisoners are locked in their cells at this time.'

'Oopsie.' 428 made a comical face of regret. 'What can I say other than that my cell door just kind of fell open? They do that around me. It's magic.' Was he laughing at me? 'I'm like the man who bends spoons. Only you'd choose to sit next to me on a bus.'

'You have broken four rules—' I stopped, and realised I didn't sound at all angry. It was as though I had forgotten all about who Prisoner 428 really was, and what he'd done. I started again, shouting this time. 'Listen to me, 428. You have broken *five* different rules of The Prison – if you include not addressing me by my proper title.'

'Well, yes, so you've said, sir.' 428 nodded, a little bored. 'Tell you what, I'll just wander back to my cell, shall I, and try and get some shut-eye?' He turned on his heel and started to walk away, then stopped. 'If you don't mind me saying so, I think you could do with some rest too. You're looking a little pasty.'

'428! You will address me as Sir!' I thundered.

428 just turned and walked steadily away, waving a hand at me distractedly. 'Get some sleep, sir. You're

going to need it,' he said, and was gone.

I stood there for a moment, shaking with rage.

The Custodian beeped, wanting to know if I wished it to follow 428 and restrain him. I shook my head. Well, let him have his little victory.

Everyone liked Guardian Donaldson. She was everything Bentley wasn't. Donaldson was a small, slightly plump woman and she was always bustling and smiling.

Her cheeriness masked a shrewdness. People assumed that Donaldson was a soft touch, but she was, if anything, more of a stickler for the rules than Bentley. The thing was, when Donaldson caught people out, they'd be more likely to hold up their hands and chuckle ruefully, 'You got me.' Bentley's sheer correctness meant that she was feared. Donaldson was treated a little like a favourite teacher.

The only person who Donaldson was reserved around was Prisoner 428. I'm not sure if Bentley had had a word with her (the two were very close), or if she was just a shrewd judge of character.

I saw Donaldson and 428 talking one day on a monitor. I didn't hear what 428 was saying but I heard Donaldson's withering response: 'If you stopped trying so hard not to fit in, you'd get along here just fine.'

*

Prisoner 428 made a friend. Bentley informed me of this fact. I pretended not to really be bothered, but I was already crackling with excitement. She leaned over my tablet to activate the cameras, and I noticed again that Bentley didn't really smell of anything. Just soap. This wasn't really remarkable, it was just that there should be a smell. I remembered my wife leaning over me to show me some gossip on a TransNet blog, and there would always be a smell. Funnily, I couldn't remember what my wife's perfume smelt like. It had been so long.

Bentley stepped back, and I hastily dismissed the idea, the very notion, of her perfume. I was the Governor, after all. Governors do not sniff the air like poets in spring. Instead I looked sternly at the screen. The feed was from one of the cameras on board a Custodian, stationed at the edge of the canteen. 428 was standing eating from a bowl with a spoon. Next to him was the weary figure of 317, a tiny old man. Poor Lafcardio.

428: *You'd think they'd give us chairs.*

317: *You get used to it, Doctor.*

428: *But if they gave us chairs we wouldn't need to get used to it.*

317: *And a table.*

428: *Yes, a table. A table and chairs.*

317: *I've always thought standing up to eat harms the*

digestion.

428: Food should be enjoyed. Not wolfed down like we're in a hurry for a meeting.

317: Quite. We don't have meetings. Not here.

428: Did you used to?

317: Oh, dear me, Doctor. In my old life? So many. My day was full of them. Looking back, I think I would have preferred longer lunches.

428: Paris. Always good for a lunch. It's not lunch unless you're in Paris and it's gone on for so long that they're tapping the 'We're Closed' sign meaningfully against the door. And coughing discreetly. Ah, no one does a discreet cough like your Parisian waiter. Ever been?

317: No. Paris sounds like a lovely world. You've spoken of it before.

428: When all this is over, I'll take you, Lafcardio. How about that?

317: You have a rare sense of humour. I like that.

428: Not as much as you'd like a rare steak. Or even steak tartare. That's something worth getting indigestion for.

317: Have you, ah, finished your porridge?

428: Oh... this? Porridge, eh? No, I've not even started it.

317: Are you going to?

428: No. Have it. I'll keep the spoon.

317: Are you sure? I'm so embarrassed to ask, but the

portions…

428: *Be my guest. Have the bowl. I'll keep the spoon. I've never been one for food.* [an absurd lie] *Now then, the question is whether we'd eat somewhere in the Marais or the Flea Market for lunch, do the second-hand bookstalls along the Seine and then on to the Terminus Nord for a late dinner. The waiters there dress like penguins and they do things with eggs that would make a chicken blush…*

317: *Actually, Doctor, could you be quiet? Just for a moment. I'm trying to eat this porridge.*

428: *Horrid, isn't it?*

317: *Unspeakable.*

[a pause]

317: *There. Have your bowl back. I didn't lick it clean. That would be undignified.*

428: *And the porridge doesn't deserve it. The moment I leave here, I can tell you I'm going to be quite catty on TripAdvisor.*

317: *Would you like to see my library, Doctor? Well, I say 'my' library, but none of us have possessions any more. Although, naturally, as hardly anyone else uses it, you could, in all honesty argue that—*

428: *Lafcardio, take me to your library. They've ruined tables, chairs and food. I'd love to see what they do to books…*

I watched the two of them shuffle away, exchanging

furtive glances with their fellow prisoners. For a moment, my memory tugged, wondering what it would be like to go to Paris with those two. It sounded like a nice place.

Surprisingly, it had taken me a moment to recall Lafcardio. A harmless enough old man, he'd taken to the prison regime calmly, almost as though the university he taught at had just suffered severe cutbacks. He was an old friend, one of the ones it wasn't worth breaking.

There were people like 428, people who, for their own good, had to be broken. And then there were those like 317 who just didn't need it. They'd already meekly submitted. Further cruelty seemed pointless. Unless, of course, it had a very good purpose.

Bentley glanced at me, waiting for me to speak, to pass comment. I felt I had to say something. Just to get into her good books.

'Oh, I know, 428's guilty of at least three minor Protocol violations and technically he's on hunger strike. But this is a good sign, Bentley. He's passing from anger to…'

'Acceptance?' Bentley seemed almost mocking.

'Well, ah…' I found her attempt at irony unsettling. 'At least, here we have the first signs of 428 coming to terms with his reality rather than denying it absolutely. And 317 is a good associate for him to have. Someone who embodies conformity. 428 can learn a lot from him.'

'That's very good, sir. But what if 317 were to learn a lot from 428?'

Bentley's notion brought me up sharp. She was always right. I hated that.

The Custodian-Cam in the library sprang into life. The lights here were dark – just bright enough to allow prisoners to see the titles of the books but not bright enough to encourage prolonged reading. The place was also kept marginally colder than the rest of the Prison. Climates were carefully controlled in the communal areas. The only room colder than the library was the swimming pool. It is amazing how easily people can be manipulated by only the smallest variations in temperature.

One mistake in the early days of the Prison Protocols was that we kept the gymnasium slightly too warm and dry. The idea behind this was to promote a slight increase of weight loss and limb flexibility in order to decrease muscle injuries. In practice, the warm, arid atmosphere promoted aggression through mild dehydration. I queried this with HomeWorld and asked for normal temperature to be reinstated, but they responded that this was an interesting result. In the end I overruled them quietly and decreased the temperature to only a fraction above normal. I could not see the advantage in provoking the prisoners.

After all, I do consider them my friends.

Which brings me back to the library. As they entered, 428 was gazing around the chamber. 317 was waiting, hands clasped together expectantly. In the end, it all got a bit much for him:

> *317: Well, what do you think?*
> *428: Grim.*
> *317: Oh.*
> *428: I don't mean to be offensive.*
> *317: I'm sure.*
> *428: But really, man. I've seen a better selection in a shut-down charity shop. Actually, it smells the same.*
> *317: I see. I'm sorry to have wasted your—*
> *428: Not at all.*

428 stormed away, clearly furious. The Library Custodian swivelled to show 317 watching him go and then, slowly and sadly, walk around the shelves, patting some volumes defensively, and pulling others down, dusting them off.

So, 428 hadn't made a friend after all. Good.

An hour or so later I was busy trying to update the expenditure allocations when I heard voices. I realised I hadn't closed the video tab, and maximised it, swiftly banishing the minutiae of oxygen reprocessor catalysts.

The Library Custodian showed 317 standing in the library, waving frantically as 428 wove around him, gathering up books.

> 428: *I'm really sorry. I must apologise. I can only express my sincerest regrets for my earlier behaviour. Here, catch.*
>
> 317: *I never could catch.*
>
> 428: *Oh dear. Neither could I.*
>
> 317: *Well then, why did you throw it?*
>
> 428: *Because I live in hope of meeting someone who can catch. They'd be handy. There we go. Look, hardly any damage to the book at all. I can easily fix the spine.*
>
> 317: *What's brought about this change of heart, Doctor, may I ask? What do you want?*
>
> 428: *To make amends. To find out why. What's marvellous about this sad collection is that it exists at all. Am I correct?*
>
> 317: *Well, yes. Initially the idea was that all prisoners would have access to books via the TransNet link. But, when that proved—*
>
> 428: *Slower than sending a text message in Somerset, yes…*
>
> 317: *Well, I took it upon myself. I went to see the Governor.*
>
> 428: *You're a brave man.*

[He pulled a face and I bristled a bit.]

317: He was very understanding, actually. I explained that we had little to read. He approached the HomeWorld Authorities, who regretted that nothing, alas could be done. But the Governor – well…

428: Are you going to make me like him?

317: A bit. Perhaps. Together, we approached the prison population, and asked if any of them had brought physical books with them as possessions that they would be willing to loan. It was agreed that any books in the personal valuables store could be donated as well. Also, the Guardians were allowed to pass on books that they no longer required to the library, which was very kind of them.

428: Yes. Funny that. You don't really think of them as readers.

317: On the contrary. One of them, Guardian Donaldson, actually discovered a loophole. Obviously, our relatives could not send us books.

428: Oh no. Perish the thought of that.

317: But Donaldson could order up books and have them sent to her by shuttle. And then, so long as the Guardians read them, they could then—

428: Be passed on to the library. Good old Donaldson. I like the sound of him.

317: You can meet later. She's rather lovely.

428: Oh, she? Right. Of course. Her! That Donaldson. Yes. A woman who likes books. The best kind.

317: Very much so. She spent a huge amount of her salary on them. She even discovered that a fair amount of the library at the university I lecture at — sorry, used to lecture at — was being… disposed of for a reasonable sum. So she ordered that. Pretty much filled a shuttle.

428: Oh. Is this going to have an unhappy ending? I'm not sure how I feel about those.

317: No, no. Well. Not exactly. Someone in shipping queried this. But only after they'd been despatched. The Governor, actually much to his regret, was forced to act. For all his… peculiarities, he means well. Reluctantly, he closed off the loophole. Well, some of it. Guards can still donate books to us. Just not whole libraries.

428: Which is silly. You're supposed to have access to books.

317: Well, yes. The Governor did try and raise that, I believe.

428: [a long sigh that I could hear from my office] How did that go?

317: Oh, badly. A new sub-contractor looked at installing private TransNet terminals that would give us fast access. Our relatives could pay for the bandwidth. But then, of course, the media back on HomeWorld found out that they were effectively charging us for reading… and, in the face of the outcry… the plan was scrapped.

428: *Rather than just give you a nicer modem that worked?*

317: *HomeWorld's funny like that. But then, that's why I'm in prison.*

428: *So, what you're telling me that all of these books – these marvellous, shoddy, tatty, and frequently unreadable books – are the result of human ingenuity and kindness? Of prisoners and guards working together to make life a tiny bit more bearable?*

317: *Yes. I even have this Custodian here – [clang!] allocated to do the filing. In the early days it just did it alphabetically, but I've recently taught it proper library filing.*

428: *The ancient art of the Dewey Decimal?*

317: *Quite so.*

428: *Marvellous. The whole really is greater than the sum of its parts. Tell you what, my amazing Lafcardio, I'm going to celebrate this by borrowing one of these books and reading it. Let's see... Jeffrey Archer? Goodness me. Perhaps not. 'Moll Flanders, now a television series starring...' Good grief. Just how old are these books? The selection here is completely random.*

317: *A lot of HomeWorld's books were shipped out as unwanted ballast from Old Old Earth. In return for minerals. They're all very weary junk.*

428: *'Unwanted ballast?' That's a terrible thing to say about books. You may as well heat an orphanage with them. Imagine that – Earth's discarded ballast becomes your precious archive. And here we go... 'I Hate Mondays by Garfield'. Always got to love a book by a cat. This will be brilliant. I'll take it.*

317: Well, if you insist.

428: I do. Hello! [The Library Custodian is tapped.] *I'm borrowing this little book, tin donkey. Hope that's OK. And you, have a good day, 317.*

317: I will Doctor.

428: Thank you Lafcardio. You know what you've done? You've given me hope. And you. [He taps the robot again.] *You keep up the good work.*

'What's he up to?' Bentley had appeared and was watching over my shoulder. I jumped, despite myself, spilling a cup of tea. We became lost for a few moments in a flurry of cleaning up and rescuing paperwork.

'You really don't have to do this,' I assured her.

'It's fine,' she said. But then she would. She was, I noticed, using my draft report to soak up a massive spillage. I would have stopped her, but that seemed churlish.

A minute or two passed of fussing and tutting and then we stood back to admire our handiwork.

'I I suppose I could have asked a Custodian to take care of it. But it would simply have set fire to the desk.'

Bentley didn't laugh, but then again, she didn't

argue. A small victory. 'My apologies, I'm sure, for disturbing you, Governor.'

'Not at all.' I decided I could afford to be magnanimous. After all, this might prove a check to that unfortunate habit of hers of sneaking into my office unannounced. She never knocked. In many ways, sodden progress reports aside, this was a bonus. So, with a rueful shake of the head, I changed the subject.

'Not at all, not at all – you were as fascinated by the Doctor and – by 428 and 317 as I was, weren't you?' I tried to sound open and inviting. I noticed that Bentley had gone back to not quite looking at me. Shame.

Bentley's eyes were fixed on the screen showing 317 pottering around his empty library, fussing over his sorry collection of books, rearranging them and talking to them like pets.

'What's 428 up to? That's my question,' I said. 'Could there be something hidden in that library that he needs, eh?'

'I think he merely needs a friend,' said Bentley.

'What?' I asked her. And then I thought about it. 'Oh.'

We continued to watch 317 in the library.

Bentley coughed delicately. 'With your permission, Governor, I have a suggestion…'

*

'No manacles this time, eh?' 428 was louder than most people I encountered here. Despite being escorted in the grip of two Custodians, he seemed to almost saunter into the room. Like he didn't really care what impression he made, as though he wouldn't be here the rest of his life, as though he would simply one day stroll away and never give us a backward glance. Well, I was going to help him come to ground. With a bump.

'No, no manacles, 428,' I assured him, leaning back expansively. 'Please sit down.'

'Oh, this is an honour,' he shrugged himself free of the Custodians and settled himself in the chair. He looked around the room. 'This is *nice*, isn't it. Yes, *nice*.' He was somehow being sardonic. I could sense italics around much of what he said. 'Your flowers need watering.'

'They don't, alas, flourish here. Not as a rule.'

428 clucked. 'Lack of sunlight. Lack of proper gravity. Lack of... well, anything that really encourages living things to really live. Do you like it here?'

I blinked. 'It is not my duty to like it. It is my duty to obey the Protocols and ensure that everyone here lives harmoniously.'

428 had stopped listening halfway through the sentence. 'Do you miss it back home?'

I spread out my hands candidly. 'I can barely

remember that. I cannot return to HomeWorld. This is my home now. Believe me, 428, once you become used to it, it has a certain tranquillity.'

428 was looking at me. He was looking straight at me. Unconsciously, I wanted to turn away, but instead I set my gaze and smiled.

'How are you enjoying escaping?' I asked him. He had very much continued to do so, wandering the prison with the casualness of a feline. He had even disabled, briefly, the Custodian we had placed outside his door, waking it up only on his return with a cheery tap and a wave. 428 was not taking The Prison seriously. That would change.

428 had begun humming, so I repeated the question. 428 gave it every appearance of serious consideration, and then he leaned forward, candidly. 'As you said, it's a hobby, really, sir. After all, every man must have a hobby. The lower security levels, they're the easy bits. It's getting beyond a certain point, that's really tricky. But I'll get there. Honestly, if you hadn't incinerated Clara's mobile, I could have shown you Candy Crush. Now that's annoying.'

'Clara?'

'Clara.' He did not want to discuss it further. So I felt perfectly comfortable in not telling him about his female visitor. Good. A weak spot. I made a note of it. 'I'll buy her a new one when I get out,' He shuddered. 'The Dalek Emperor is nothing compared to your average mobile phone sales assistant. Ach, maybe I'll just stay here the rest of my life, eh? Less bother.'

I leaned forward. 'You will stay here the rest of your life, 428. You appear to be having trouble accepting that.'

428 nodded. 'I do. So I do.'

'Well, I'm going to help you,' I told him.

'Thumbscrews?' he rubbed his hands with excitement.

'No. What do you take us for? I'm going to make you an offer.'

'Really?'

'Tables and chairs.'

428 looked at me curiously.

'You expressed a wish that the canteen had tables and chairs. Here is my bargain. If you stay in your cell during lockdown for the next three days and nights… then the canteen may have tables and chairs.'

'You're bribing me with furniture?' 428 appeared delighted, as though this had never been tried before.

'Tables and chairs. You have my word, 428.'

He nodded. 'All right then. We have a bargain.' Then his face set hard as ice. 'Just one thing. My name. It's not binding unless you call me by my name.'

The request annoyed me. It clearly wasn't a real name. It was little better than 428. And, yet considering the things that had been done in it, it hurt me to do it.

'Doctor,' I smiled sweetly. 'Stay in your cell when you're supposed to for three days and nights and the canteen will have tables and chairs.'

428 leaned across the table and shook my hand, staring into my eyes. There was a silence for a long moment, broken only by the Custodians going to Warning Mode.

'Done,' said 428.

5

The first two days and nights of 428's agreement passed without incident. I mentioned this to Bentley, but she set her lips thinly and left to file a TransNet report. And then, on the third night…

No one knew exactly how the fire started. But somewhere in the book stack, between biographies and fiction. Paper smoulders and smokes first, which should have set off an alarm. But there was no alarm. Not until the first book burst neatly into flame and then the fire spread. In Dewey Decimal order.

The news spread around the Prison just as fast. Even though it was the middle of the night and everyone was locked down, still the news spread. Gossip travels faster than fires here. The alarms helped, rousing people from troubled dreams to smoke-filled corridors.

Prisoner 428 appeared at the window-grille of his cell, talking directly to the Custodian guarding the corridor. It was one of the newer models. One fitted with a basic vocal system.

'The situation is under control.'

'What situation?'

'There is a fire. The situation is under control.'

'Where is the fire? Where!' 428 was alert, already suspicious.

'The Prison library.'

428 stood at the window of his cell, a caged lion snarling. Only, I watched the footage again later and, actually, he didn't snarl or shout. And yet, if you'd asked me, I'd have said he'd done both. He just stood there, quite calmly.

'Where is Lafcardio?' he asked eventually.

The Custodian did not reply.

428 repeated his question. And then, with a weary sigh of resignation, vanished from the window of his cell. A moment later, the door popped open and the Custodian's camera went blank. As it did so, 428 muttered something bitterly.

'Tables and chairs.'

When 428 arrived outside the library, a phalanx of Custodians had gathered, forming a barrier to the open door belching smoke.

'Aren't you doing anything?' he demanded.

Bentley appeared, smiling at him soothingly. 'Not in your cell, 428?'

'And what are you doing about the fire?'

'A pity.' Bentley was calm as a new siren sounded. 'Flashpoint alarm. Don't worry. Vacuum Protocols are activating automatically. In less than thirty seconds, the library will be sealed off and the air vented into space.'

428 listened to what she said, nodding intently. 'And what about Lafcardio?'

'He was in his cell when the alarm went off.' Bentley shrugged.

'Yes. In his cell. The cell that isn't locked at night because he can be trusted.' 428 was already pushing past her. 'In his cell. When the alarm went off telling him his precious library was burning. In his cell. Flashpoint alarm. Less than thirty seconds, you said?'

The Doctor vanished into the smoke.

Twenty-six seconds later, the Vacuum Protocols activated. Space filled with a brief puff of flame that twinkled until it went beyond the atmospheric bubble that surrounded the asteroid. Then the flame went out. Floating away from The Prison were the first things ever to escape from it. Tumbling bundles of burnt books, some falling in groups, some just single floating pages, moving off into space for ever. *The Woman in White* bumped against *The Da Vinci Code* and, as if by mutual agreement, edged away from *Shall We Tell the President?*

*

428 stood on the other side of the blast door, and exhaled quickly. His face was blackened by soot, but he seemed unscathed by his heroics. Lafcardio was a tiny crumpled heap in his arms. 428 lowered him gently to the floor, and then quickly began to administer artificial resuscitation.

This had not been supposed to happen. I'm sure this hadn't been supposed to happen. Bentley's shock seemed genuine. She stepped up to 428. 'Let a Custodian take care of him,' but he shrugged her angrily away.

He worked on the body like an expert and for a long time it seemed futile. Then Lafcardio gasped, spluttered and looked dazedly up into 428's face. 'Well, this is certainly unexpected,' he croaked, then coughed. His cough did not stop.

428 hoisted him up into a sitting position and then waited until the hacking fit subsided slightly. He turned to Bentley. 'Get him a glass of water, won't you? Oxygen would be lovely, but water would be just darling.'

Startled, Bentley started to obey before stopping herself relaying the order to a Custodian. She turned back to watch 428, folding her arms and observing him.

'I'm so sorry,' whispered 428 to Lafcardio.

'My books?' croaked the man.

'They're all gone,' said 428. 'I'm sorry. It's all my

fault.'

'How…? How…?' Lafcardio was crying, tears running through the soot on his face. He didn't appear to have listened to 428 at all. 'I tried to stop it… But the flames… So difficult.'

428 held him close and looked directly up at my camera.

'Someone,' 428's tone was grim, 'was trying to teach me a lesson.'

'We had an agreement,' I said to 428 when I arrived later. 'You were not to leave your cell.'

'You're going to be childish, aren't you?' 428, if anything, appeared to be the childish one. He was leaning against the wall, having reluctantly surrendered Lafcardio to a Medical Custodian. He gestured to the sealed library. 'This was all your idea, wasn't it?'

'Are you accusing me of vandalising prison property?' I thundered. 'If you wish, an inquiry into this accident will take place…'

'Oh, spare yourself the bother.' 428 was viciously bored. He yawned and looked about to go, but then he spun back, his fingers jabbing at my face. 'Listen to me, you stupid little man—'

'I- I am the Governor here. I will be accorded respect!' I rallied. 'I am taller than you.'

'You're tiny. Small. Minuscule. Not worth the effort.

The effort of all this,' He waved around at the room and then pointed at me. 'Listen to me. You never burn books. Even rubbish ones. Especially not when they're the delight of a harmless man. And why? Your plan went horribly wrong. You could have killed him – just to teach me a lesson. You could have had that on your conscience.'

'I assure you my conscience is clear.'

'Is it?' The full fury of 428 was like being trapped in a freezer. I looked away. 'I thought not. If any of this is to be worthwhile... Oh, never mind.' He shrugged, his shoulders rising and falling as mountains. 'Nighty night. I'm off to my cell. Unless...'

Bentley appeared at 428's side smoothly. 'If I may point out, 428...'

'Ah.' 428 seemed unimpressed. 'It's the Little Match Girl.'

Bentley's silken smile didn't waver. 'May I remind you, Prisoner 428, that you have broken curfew, and a personal agreement with the Governor?'

428 arched an eyebrow slowly and he started to applaud. It was slow and sarcastic. 'Please tell me it's solitary confinement.'

'Indeed.' Bentley refused to appear unsettled.

'Splendid.' 428 rubbed his hands together. 'Because I can't stand the sight of any of you at the moment. I fancy a rest from all of your faces. Take me to my new caravan. Oh...' He turned to Bentley. 'And do say sorry to Lafcardio from me. Won't you?'

Bentley nodded.

'Good,' 428 said strolling towards the waiting Custodians. 'Because I don't think he'll get an apology from you lot otherwise.'

We'd placed a camera in his new cell, but it didn't show anything much. Simply 428 sat, motionless. With his back to the camera.

For hours.

The girl came back. She was standing on the landing pad, hair neatly swept back. Her clothes were identical, only covered in dots of paint. She was holding a placard.

'Oh,' she said. 'Hello!' She stuck out her hand. 'Don't shake it,' she said. 'Paint's still wet. And also, electric field.'

'Yes,' I said.

'I knew you'd come.' Clara seemed pleased with herself.

'Well, I am only mandated to make one visit. I may, of course, come out a second time.'

'You'll come out loads more,' she assured me.

'Well,' I chuckled, 'that's purely at my discretion.'

'You really are a pompous ass,' smiled Clara. 'You'd like my headmaster.'

'Ah,' I said. 'This is how you're going to win

clemency for the Doctor.'

'Uh-huh,' she said. 'That and the signs. Do you like them?'

She waved the placard. 'FREE THE DOCTOR,' it said, decorated with various coloured handprints.

'Class 2B made them,' she said. She turned around the placard. On the back it said, 'SAVE DOT COT'. I looked at her.

'Oh, yes, 2A got a leetle bit confused. Dot Cotton. Famous cockney chimney. Doesn't matter. The broomstick was leant to me by Danny. He's another teacher at the school. No, wait, he doesn't matter.' Clearly a boyfriend. Did I feel jealous about this? Oddly, no.

'Are you all right?' I asked.

'Yes. Er. Why?'

'You seem nervous.'

'Ah, yes. Well, I'm in two places at once at the moment.' Clara's face fell. 'It doesn't matter. How's the Doctor getting on?'

'Prisoner 428 is being cared for in accordance with agreed Protocols.'

'Agreed Protocols? I just bet he loves that.' Clara made a face.

'No, he doesn't.'

'Thought not.' She made a great play of trying to seem casual. 'Listen,' she said. 'Can I... can I give you something?'

'Is it a petition?' I sighed. 'I can accept them, but not gifts or letters for prisoners.' I was disappointed by Clara. Bored, I pointed to a gap in the chain fence. There was a silver box fitted to it. 'If you so wish.' I'd really hoped better of her. 'Place what you have in the box.'

Clara hesitated. 'It's vitally important you read this. You'll understand.'

'Painted for me by Class 2B?'

'Well, no. Well, all right, a lot of important stuff and just the one painting. But it's quite nice. And 2B made me promise. After the Doctor came and did balloon animals one afternoon. Anyway, that's not the point.' She pulled a bundle from her satchel and placed it in the box. 'You've got to read this. Hey, where are you going?'

'Well,' I said, 'I assure you that I will read your material. Once the seven systems necessary to transfer these objects over have been deactivated. Which requires oversight and screening. Then, if the items have passed that screening, then the contents of the Honesty Box will be passed—'

'Honesty Box?'

'Yes. That's what it's called.'

'Even your post gets censored?'

'Screened.'

Clara screwed her face up in fury. 'I bet all you end up with is a painting of some dogs playing football.

It's quite good, although they glued on the football. It's made out of tinfoil. So, if it falls off you may find the whole purpose of the painting a bit mystifying. A lot of lost dogs. Mystifying and pointless.' She underlined the last words.

I bowed formally. 'Then I look forward to seeing it,' I told her.

'How's the Doctor doing?' she shouted as I turned away.

'Oh, surviving,' I said, and left her alone on the landing pad, waving her placard.

Guardian Donaldson broke up the fight in the canteen.

203… she'd always been a bit of a bruiser. Abesse, that had been her name. She'd been a mercenary on the losing side during the HomeWorld Revolution and had always seemed rather sour about it. Due to the wrong name being on her pay cheque that month, the new President had sent her here. I'm not sure I blamed her for being bitter. Not really.

She'd settled into Prison life just as some people settled into an assignment they didn't much care for. She had an eye on the end of it, I could tell. Which seemed ironic because, as I'm sure you know, no one ever leaves here.

In some ways, it was surprising that Prisoner 428 didn't notice her bearing down on him. 203 was very tall and quite striking. I think I'd have called her beautiful if she wasn't so hard-faced. Her hair was still cut sharply and fashionably, as though she was ready to throw on a dress and go to a party. Just waiting for the call to somewhere much more interesting.

Personally, I thought it was a huge waste having a mercenary of her skills here. By definition, she'd be just as happy working for the new regime. But the government had been very black-and-white about these things.

In The Prison, 203 occasionally acted as an informal, intermediary justice system. This is a polite way of saying Abesse attacked people who annoyed her.

Hence the reason why 428 was suddenly flying through the air.

He picked himself up from among the feet of prisoners who had hurriedly stepped back. He shook himself down, and patted imaginary creases out of his uniform.

'If you'd wanted my porridge, you just needed to ask,' he said.

Abesse stood over him. Towered over him.

'So… Not about porridge?' ventured 428.

He didn't have time to protect himself before he smacked into a wall with a crack and a thud.

I noticed the Custodians were not reacting, and wondered if I should dispatch some Guardians. But then again, this was Prisoner 428. This would do him some good. Sometimes we all turned a blind eye to 203. She was a useful asset.

The crumpled heap that was 428 sat up and waved gently at 203.

'You're cross with me. I get that. But I don't get entirely why. If I have to guess it will be tedious, and believe me, I'm only too aware that my manner in these situations can occasionally come across as a bit unfortuna—'

428 spun quite a long way along the floor this time before coming to a stop.

Then he sprang up, smiling.

203 charged at him

428 didn't move. Well, hardly moved. Just a single digit, waggling somewhere near 203's shoulder as she swept down onto him.

Prisoner 203 suddenly slid to the floor with a groan.

'You're lucky,' 428 stood over her. 'I don't use Venusian Aikido much these days. And rarely on ladies. Not as a rule. But then again —' a wink — 'You're no lady.'

203's eyes sprang open, glaring at him. She struggled to get up.

428 considered her. 'You're cross with me. I get that. Is it because of the library, because of poor Lafcardio, or because you didn't get any tables or chairs in here? Or… actually, is it all three? Because, put together like

that, I'll admit, it does look rather bad.'

203 sprang to her feet, snarling.

And then, strangely, slid to the floor again.

This time she did not get up.

'That was more of a tap, really,' 428 muttered sheepishly. Then he crouched by 203 and whispered something in her ear.

By this time, Guardian Donaldson had arrived to break up the fight. She surveyed the wreckage with typically dryness. She found 428 as unamusing as I did. But 428 seemed pleased to see her. 428 helped 203 up. 'Her name is Abesse,' he informed Donaldson, 'and I'm afraid she's a little shaken up.' Abesse was leaning woozily against a wall. 'Do be careful with her. Her inner ear is temporarily a little off so you'll find her sense of balance won't answer questions for a day or so.'

In hindsight, placing Prisoner 203 next to Lafcardio in the medical centre was a mistake.

The next time I saw 203, a few days later, she and the... Prisoner 428 were heading off to the crafting workshop, a place where prisoners devoted themselves to hobby-craft. The two of them looked, if you will excuse the expression, as thick as thieves.

Quite how the seal to the library was breached, I don't know. We only found out about it later. When I asked

428 where he'd got the wood from.

'Don't you like the tables?' he'd asked, hurt.

We were standing in the canteen. Which was now full of tables. And benches.

'We repainted,' 428 explained. 'Yellow was a bit provoking. Pink has a calming effect. They discovered this on Alcatraz.' He leaned over me, indicating a bench.

'Do take a seat,' he'd insisted. 'Well, not on that pew. It wobbles. Just a bit.'

'Where...' My mouth was dry. 'Where did you get the wood?'

'Oh, well.' 428 looked decidedly casual. 'There were all those shelves in the library. Empty shelves. No books now, you see. And Abesse and I thought that... well... she is a wonder with a handsaw.' He beamed, pleased.

I just stood there. Stood there as prisoners started filing in for the morning meal, collecting their porridge and sitting down at the tables. They were all smiling. Not talking, just beaming. Abesse stood at the back of them all. Arms folded. Watching me. Waiting for a challenge.

'Sometimes,' smiled 428, 'it's not the final destination that counts, but how you get there. And sometimes both the journey and the destination are most rewarding.'

He reached over to something on the table and

handed it to me. It was a pot, with a plant in it.

'It's a rosebush,' he said. 'I know you like flowers. I grew it in the hydroponics centre.'

'But Prisoners aren't allowed in the—'

The Doctor shrugged. 'And isn't that a shame? Stick it on your desk. Water it. Enjoy.'

I stared at it. Little red buds were already showing. Helen had always loved roses. I wanted to say something. But I couldn't thank the Doctor. I just couldn't. That would have made his victory complete. Instead I held the plant to me. Already I could smell it.

The Doctor turned and started to stride away.

'Not staying—' I stopped. My tone had been abrupt, showing how much he'd got to me. So I stopped. I did not say 'to enjoy your victory'. Instead I managed: 'To enjoy your porridge?'

428 turned, and shuddered theatrically. 'No. I can't stand the food here. But don't worry. That's on my list.'

He smiled at me and was gone.

Bentley and I looked at each other. She was almost staring right into my eyes.

'He's winning, isn't he?' I said.

Bentley didn't answer. She looked away.

There was a power fluctuation that night. Six minutes and twelve seconds. I'd almost forgotten them. Bentley and I argued about it, quite firmly.

'Level 7,' she was saying. 'You have to isolate Level 7 now and claw back resources.'

'I can't do that,' I protested.

'The Protocols say it's the only way.'

I knew, more or less, that she was right. Level 7 was self-contained. They'd be fine. For a bit. But I just didn't like the idea.

Which was when the red lights faded and the alarm stopped.

We'd escaped again.

After the alarm stopped, two people were found where they shouldn't be.

One was 428. He was standing over the body of Guardian Donaldson.

'I know what this looks like,' said 428 as Bentley hit him. 'I was trying to find the source of the alarm… and so was she.'

But Bentley carried on hitting him. She was crying.

Curiously, 428 put his arms around her and held her. 'I rather liked Donaldson too,' he said. 'I am sorry for your loss.'

I visited 428 in the solitary cell. It was more of a cupboard, but he seemed unconcerned by his surroundings.

'How is Bentley?' he asked.

I shook my head. 'That doesn't matter. 428, why did

you kill Donaldson?'

'I didn't.' He seemed annoyed I'd even asked. 'We were both looking for the source of the alarm. I'm afraid she was more successful than me. She found it and it killed her.'

'What did?'

428 shrugged. He leaned forward to tap me on the nose, but the force wall crackled menacingly around his hand. 'There's something in this prison that even you don't know about, Governor.'

'You expect me to believe that?'

428 spread his arms out again. 'Did I have a weapon on me? Come to that, and given the state of Donaldson, did I have all the weapons on me?'

I glared at him. There were times when there was no place for flippancy.

I left him in solitary. He could rot there as far as I was concerned.

Donaldson had been religious. Or, at least, her family was. And so their beliefs had made it onto her personnel forms. According to custom, her body would be placed in its bier and rest in the chapel overnight before being disposed of the following dawn (Relative HomeWorld time).

Someone would watch over Donaldson during the night. I decided it would be me. I was glad the casket was closed. It meant I could sit and feel sorry for myself.

I hadn't really known Donaldson very well. I'd liked her. I currently felt terribly responsible for her. But that was all. That and a terrible sense of guilt stretching eight hours ahead of me.

There was a gentle cough and 428 slid into the chair next to me.

For a moment I ignored him. I really couldn't think of anything else to do.

428 didn't seem in a hurry to speak either.

We just sat there, staring at her casket in silence. I could tell, from the anguish on his face, that he felt as guilty about this as I did. Not guilty as in he'd murdered her, but guilty as in terribly responsible for her death. I wondered if the guilt, his guilt, my guilt, would ever feel better. I glanced across at 428, trying to work out if he still felt crushed under the guilt of his victims. If he could come here and sit by me… Well, he must do, surely.

We sat there for a little while more. I stopped checking my watch every five minutes and gradually a stillness settled over us. Donaldson's casket, Prisoner 428 and me. Lit only by the candles, the air perfumed gently by the artificial flowers I'd ordered up from synthesis, and much more so by the flowers 428 had brought. He'd found real lilies (I have no idea how), but soon the air reeked of them.

Suddenly, I realised it was almost dawn. The night

had drifted by in its gentle melancholy. 428 stood up and bowed to the coffin.

'Doctor…' I said and then paused. I couldn't bring myself to thank him.

'Tell Bentley I am sorry,' 428 said to me, his voice soft. 'And, just so you know, solitary is just as easy to get out of.' He smiled sadly, patted me on the shoulder, and then left.

The Oracle blipped me from Level 7. His face was pulled into a fat comedy of dolour.

'I hear you have had a tragedy,' he intoned, his fingers waggling upside down. 'Most regrettable. Most sad. Most… purple.'

'Is there a point to this?' Normally I did a better job of hiding how irritated I was by the Oracle.

'Oh, am I interrupting?' the Oracle slapped one hand with another, 'Silly me, I should have foreseen that… I wouldn't dream of interrupting you on such a serious occasion, only… what with your sad events… the aura reaches even down here. Such sad thoughts impinge on the clarity of my visions.' I couldn't believe it – the fool was blaming us for messing around with his phoney clairvoyance. It wasn't even as though he was a real mystic – simply a well-informed gossip. But he wasn't harmless either. I thought putting him charge of Level 7 was a decision made in rather bad taste.

As though answering some apologetic comment from me, the Oracle held up his hands. 'There's really no need to say sorry for the interference in my visions! It's most regrettable, but these things happen. However, rest assured, my dear Governor, that you are not to blame.' The way he said it, he clearly did blame me. 'It is simply that…' He pressed his fingers into his forehead, sinking them into the flesh around his temples, 'Ah, yes, such a pity. I should be able to see clearly ahead, but as it is, with so much interference there is a cloud… through a veil of burgundy thoughts…' He kneaded away at his eyebrows, and then assumed a face of benevolent piety. 'I can tell you this. Soon you will have to consider the fate of Level 7. Miserable wretches that we are.' He wagged a finger at me and terminated the blip.

Clara was back on the landing pad. And she was holding up a new placard.

'This time I painted it myself,' she said, with a shrug. 'I think if I'd got the kids to do it I'd have ended up on a list. And not a good list.'

'I see,' I said, looking at the placard. 'And in what way do you expect me not to interpret this as a terrorist threat?'

'Oh,' she glanced up at the placard. 'Did you get the documents from last time?'

I scratched my head. To be honest, So many pieces

of paper came my way. 'I'm not sure. I don't think so.'

'Well, honestly,' she sighed. 'It's a conspiracy.'

'Maybe,' I said, trying to be helpful. 'Maybe I'm just really behind on my paperwork.'

'You seriously expect me to believe that?'

'We have had a lot on,' I said. I could hear how tired my voice sounded.

She rolled her eyes. 'The Doctor is very important.'

'That may be. But he is Prisoner 428. We have 427 other prisoners, all of whom are just as important to us. He is being looked after and he is being cared for in accordance with the Protocols. Please believe me. If you have questions about the judicial process that sent him here, I urge you to pursue them with HomeWorld.'

'I can't,' said Clara and glanced over her shoulder. 'I really can only get lifts here. My, er, transport doesn't like me much.'

'Pardon? Your shuttle?'

Clara pulled a face. 'It's temperamental. It used to hate me. Now it just kind of tolerates me. Home or here. That's it. And not necessarily in the right order.'

'Got you.' I didn't get her. She seemed to be talking gibberish.

'Honestly,' she rolled her eyes. 'One day it'll break down and I'll end up stranded in one place. Can you imagine that – oh!' she covered her mouth in embarrassment. 'Sorry about that.'

'Not at all,' I said stiffly. 'Carry on telling me all about your travels.'

'No, no,' Clara assured me. 'I'm done now I've put my foot in it. We can do politics if you'd prefer. The new President of HomeWorld is proving thoroughly unpopular. I can talk about that if you'd like.'

'I'd rather not,' I said tightly.

'Then there's always the weather…' Clara looked up at the star-filled sky, as though expecting rain.

'If you've nothing meaningful to say –' I was pleased at how acidic I sounded – 'Perhaps I'd better leave you to talk with your… craft about making other arrangements to get you home. If you will excuse me, I have a prison to run.'

'I see.'

'Clara. Do you like me?' I didn't know why I said it.

'Like you?' She looked startled. Like a jam jar had asked her how to vote.

'Never mind. I must go.' I stood up quickly, embarrassed.

'Before you do…' Clara coughed and waved her sign importantly. 'My sign. I'll read it out to you, shall I?'

'Please don't. I can read.'

'Free. The. Doctor. Or. The. Killing. Will. Start.' She paused. 'There!'

For some absurd reason she looked pleased with herself.

I just groaned. 'You're too late. The killing has already started,' I said and left her there.

Her face fell.

I didn't think I'd come out and see her again.

If I'm going to be truthful, in the lift back to my office, I did feel a little troubled at how I'd left things with Clara. A tiny nagging voice told me it would be so much easier to just be nice to her. But it was too late for that, and now my office awaited along with Bentley's judging stare. I went back in and slumped down at my desk. A Custodian brought me tea. I didn't drink it. A Custodian, possibly the same one, brought me more tea. I barely touched that. I just sat watching Clara on the camera, standing in the landing bay, patiently holding up her sign. Eventually, her arms got tired and she rubbed one and then the other. Then she marched up and down a bit. Finally, she put the sign down on the ground, huffed, and walked sadly away.

6

I felt so tired that day. That was my only excuse for everything that came after it.

There'd been two more power outages in the night, one more in the daytime, and then, just when I'd turned in for the night, another came. The worst one yet.

The siren woke me. It felt as though I'd only just put my head down, but it seemed two hours had passed. I worried that one day I'd actually drift back off and sleep through an emergency.

I pulled myself out of bed and hurried to the Control Station. Bentley was there. She actually looked tired, for once. Since Donaldson's death she'd been looking tired a lot. Several other Guardians were there – more than were strictly needed to man the workstations. They were hanging back, against the walls, out of the way of the Custodians. Was it my imagination or were the Custodians getting twitchy? There was something about the haste of their movements that seemed almost ill-at-ease.

My gaze went automatically to the Situation Clock. We'd had five minutes of this already. The day's disruptions had been fairly small by comparison – three-minuters. Little nothing emergencies. Now, we were pushing well towards six minutes. The map of the Prison plan, promising to update. But nothing was going on.

'Report?' I asked the room, hopefully.

For once Bentley didn't answer. She had vanished under a control panel, cursing. Her deputy Marla came hurrying over, holding up a plastic clipboard. 'Sir, the outage is affecting the rerouting. We can't get into the system to stabilise it.'

'Soon you will have to consider the fate of Level 7.'

The Oracle's words returned to haunt me – perhaps he wasn't a total fraud. The noise of the sirens grew. We had now slid past six minutes and work was stopping. All eyes were fixed on the board. They were slowly drifting towards me, expecting me to tell them what to do. To produce a miracle.

Bentley finally pulled herself up from under the control panel. 'There's nothing we can do, Governor,' she said, tersely admitting defeat, 'We can't hack into the system to deactivate it. Once we hit seven minutes we'll have a cascade failure.'

Bentley was the kind of person who could say 'cascade failure' without looking at all sheepish about it. She didn't even give off the impression that she'd heard it once on a training course, thought it cool, and memorised it for later use. When she said 'cascade failure' she meant it.

Thinking of what the Oracle has said, I nodded. 'Can we isolate and eject Level 7?' I asked. It was the only bit of The Prison that could be ejected. At least they'd have some chance, and it would free up critical resources. Buy us a little more time.

Marla checked a couple of icons on her clipboard. 'They'd have limited motive power and only enough oxygen for twelve hours'

I didn't care. 'That's probably twelve more hours than us. The Oracle may think of something. After all,' I smiled, 'he seems to have an opinion on everything else around here. Start the uncoupling.'

If nothing else, it gave everyone something to do.

The clock hit six minutes and forty seconds. Funny. Once we got to seven minutes, there'd be no great explosion. None of us would die. Probably the first we'd notice is the lights going a little dim. The air getting a trifle warm. The doors taking a bit longer to open. But once the cascade failure had happened, then the collapse of the prison would speed up from there. Death would creep over us. And it wouldn't be pleasant.

At six minutes and forty-five seconds, another alarm went off. The two sirens wailed at each other like courting beasts, a sound that was ugly and blocky and shrill, and then the main alarm cut out. Mercifully, the clock reset and the Prison Plan flickered, seeming to shift slightly, before finally reloading. It was as if nothing had happened.

Almost silence.

Except…

Bentley spotted it. 'Level 6. All the doors are open.' That explained the other alarm still sounding.

Level 6?

'And another thing,' sighed Bentley. '428 is out of his cell.'

Normally Bentley would deal with this. But she had remained in the Control Station, going methodically through the systems, checking off each one and ensuring its performance was optimal. Until the next time the whole thing fell over.

So I went looking for 428. I took a Custodian. Just in case.

The annoying thing was that 428's timing was dreadful. This was the worst moment to be pulling his running-around stunts. He was normally more careful. He usually slipped in and out of his cell without troubling the alarms, but this time he'd lit the board up like a festive display.

As we made our way to Level 3, I marvelled at how quiet The Prison seemed at night. Even with the alarm, there was just muttering from the cells. Clearly, they'd got used to sleeping through the alarms. I called out to reassure people that everything was under control. The thing is, I didn't know if I was lying or not. We'd been less than twenty seconds away from a slow and lingering death. With a bit of luck, most of them wouldn't have woken up.

428's cell was open and empty. A note was pinned to the door: 'Back in 5 mins. Sign for any parcels'. I did not find it funny.

The Custodian was able to trace his footsteps. They led right the way down to Level 6.

Level 6 looked wrong. If the rest of the Prison had been quiet, this was icy. There wasn't a sound. It was just one long corridor at the bottom of The Prison. We put people here we did not want to think about. I'm not proud of that, but there are some people in The Prison you just can't handle normally. When corrective therapy and normal restraint fails, then we have little option other than to drug them up and ship them down to Level 6. It was where we could forget our failures.

My Custodian sent out a worried alarm chirrup. I queried this on my clipboard and then I realised what its problem was. It was trying to connect to the other Custodians on the level but there were no other Custodians here. Normally you don't notice them. They're either housed in the walls, or gliding up and down corridors, silent and efficient. The Custodians are part of the Prison. On Level 6 there were no human Guardians – only Custodians. Even if they weren't patrolling the corridors you'd expect to find them docked in the walls. But nothing. Not a sign of one. Curious. You got so used to having them around as part of the furniture that their absence was disconcerting.

That there was no sign of the prisoners was one thing. But for the Custodians to have vanished as well was extremely odd. I looked behind, just to check that the Custodian I'd brought with me was still there. It was. The corridor back to the lift stretched away behind it. It suddenly seemed a very long way away.

And then the light at the end of the corridor flickered and went off.

Without thinking, I turned to the Custodian and ordered it to investigate. As soon as it glided off, I knew it had been a mistake to send it. But I couldn't bring myself to call it back. I just watched it smoothly passing down the corridor, listening to the slight hum as it travelled. It went into the darkness. I could still see its shape moving. I could still hear it. Or could I? I blinked, and now all I could see was darkness.

I was now on my own, and we were under threat. I blipped for help. But there was no answer from the Control Station. I was cut off.

Carefully, I reached for a cell door. It was open. Inside was empty.

I blipped up to the Control Station again. I used the code for Escaped Prisoner. The situation was getting even more serious. And, in theory, my emergency call should be carried on the core transponder. No need for complicated communications. And yet still no response.

I reached over to another cell door, a terrible suspicion forming in my mind. It was also empty. I looked around more forensically. No sign of a struggle. No facetiously helpful note.

I tried out three more cells. All of them empty. Then I backed out into the corridor. I was completely alone. My footsteps echoed.

I opened another cell door, belonging to Prisoner 37. It was also, obviously, empty. I stood, looking around. There was something wrong about the sheer emptiness of the cell, as though I was missing something. I tried to work out what it was.

It took me a while to work it out. The cell was neat. Not the neatness of someone with good habits. The entire cell had been scrupulously tidied after its occupant had left. There weren't just no signs of a struggle. There were no signs that anyone had been here for a while. How long had Prisoner 37 been missing? I was pondering this when I heard the footsteps outside. Something, someone was coming.

I did not react as the Governor of the Prison. I reacted as a frightened man, as a coward. I told you I was tired. It's the only excuse I can offer. With a frightened man's ingenuity, I slid the door closed silently and crouched low down, out of sight of the window . I felt a terrible fear, like a child's game suddenly being played in deadly earnest by grown-ups. The footsteps got closer.

I tried to work out a way of fighting back. If I pushed the door… well, would that work? Could I use the door as a weapon? Would it knock my attacker off balance, giving me a chance to…

I counted the footsteps. They were not stopping at any of the other cells. This meant that, in all probability, they weren't coming for me. They did not know I was there.

The footsteps passed my cell. I breathed out. The footsteps stopped.

They came back. They stood outside my door.

This was it. Either I somehow used the door against them or I prayed they weren't looking for me.

I breathed in, tensed up, and shoved the door. It didn't spring open, it didn't fly open. It just eased open gently. Of course. The doors had been fitted with hinges which prevented them opening too quickly.

A hand took the door. A hand opened the door.

Someone stood over me. Watching.

I found I could barely move.

It took all of my courage to look up, to open my eyes. To see…

Prisoner 428 was standing over me.

'Hello, Governor,' he said. He was wearing a sardonic smile, clearly amused at finding me huddled on the floor. His smile was so sour it was practically a grimace. 'And what's a sir like you doing crouching in a place like this?'

I launched myself at him then.

He'd caught me at my most vulnerable. But I was going to show him. I had been carefully trained in restraint procedures.

Looking back, I'd like to think I'd caught him off guard. I'd like to say he wasn't expecting it. I'd like to think I surprised him. But I'm really not sure. He seemed winded by the assault, and it was halfway down to the ground with him that I remembered how Abesse's fight with him had gone. I suddenly worried that this hadn't been the cleverest of moves.

'Seriously?' said 428.

We were both lying on the floor, half in and half out of the cell. I had him in a Subdue Lock that should have been going my way. 'Seriously? The doorframe is really digging into my back and I think you've bruised your knee. You'll probably need some liniment rubbing into it.'

The thing about 428 is that he never turns it off. That's what suddenly and hugely got to me then. That air of quiet, almost smug amusement. I once threw a surprise birthday party for my wife. I'd arranged it all really carefully, and there was absolutely, definitely, no way she could know – it was a surprise. And yet, on the walk to the house, Helen kept giving me a look, a little smile that said that she knew what was coming.

And that was it. That was what Prisoner 428 was doing now. That slight twinkle in the eyes that says 'I know what you're up to. I know what's happening. There are no surprises. Not for me.' Damn him. Damn 428. Damn the Doctor.

I started shouting then. I don't think I need record everything I said to him, but the gist of it was that I was fed up playing his games, I wanted to know what he'd done and what had happened to the prisoners.

'Actually, so do I,' said 428.

I let go of him. I stood up, gasping and winded. 428 did the same.

We stood there, warily looking at each other.

'Something rubbish has happened here,' said 428 looking up and down the corridor. 'Rubbish. It's a technical term.' He saw my look and held up his hands. 'Sorry,' he said, and seemed genuine. 'If you think I'm annoying now, you'd have hated me when I was young.'

I took a step forward, and winced. 428 was right. I had bruised my knee badly. 'So… 428.'

'Governor, sir?'

'All the prisoners on this block are missing. As are the Custodians. Where are they? What have you done with them? The only thing I find here is you. I find that suspicious.'

'And the only thing I find here is you. I also find that suspicious.' He winked. 'Touché.'

'I'm the Governor here,' I said.

'So you say,' said 428.

An uncomfortable moment passed.

'I *am* the Governor,' I protested.

'Really? Perhaps you simply look like him. And, if you are, then where is your Custodian?'

I pointed to the darkness. 'It went to investigate down there... and... didn't come back.'

'Mind you,' said 428, sitting down on the bunk. 'If you were an alien shapeshifter, you'd have a better story than that. See?' He spread out his hands. 'See how trusting I am? How quick I am to give people the benefit of the doubt? You really should try it some time. You might have fun.'

I slumped next to him on the bunk. 'Look, why did you get out of your cell?' I realised how truculent I sounded. 'Why did you trigger the alarms?'

428 leaned back and clicked his tongue. 'Normally I'm a bit subtler, aren't I? But I think we're both tired. And that alarm had been going on for over six minutes. I say that, just to sound casual and so that I'm not

letting on that it had been 6 minutes and thirty-nine seconds. Normally you can feel power being rerouted to cope with the system failure. You know, the air gets a little sticky, the gravity goes by 0.3 per cent and then by 0.8 per cent… Those little tell-tales. But this time nothing. Which meant that this time, before it ended, it was so bad your system was locked out of whatever was going on. It really needed a kick up the backdoor.'

'I'm sorry?'

'It takes an expert to open their cell door as badly as I did. I set off all the alarms, didn't I? It pulled your system out of its loop and gave it something fresh to sink its teeth into.'

'You're saying… you escaped to try and help me?'

'Yes,' admitted 428. 'And also because I fancied a walk.'

'A walk down here… to Level 6. Where… I find you. And nothing else?'

'Yes,' said the Doctor. 'I could see the breach on a diagnostic panel I in no way hacked into on my way out. If you check the logs, you'll find that the problems started down here before I left my cell. Something was opening the doors and removing the last remaining prisoners down here.'

'Unless,' I smiled, 'You'd already left your cell and the loud alert was you giving yourself some kind of alibi.'

'Sneaky.' 428 nodded. 'That's really how you think,

isn't it? I guess that's why you're the Governor and I'm the prisoner, isn't it?'

'You're mocking me.'

'Perish the thought, sir.' 428 sprang to his feet. 'Come on. Let's find out what's been going on here.'

Which was when we found out that the door was locked.

Somehow in our struggle, we'd pulled it closed and it had locked.

'How embarrassing,' chuckled the Doctor. 'Locked inside your own cells. Awkward.'

A silence settled between us.

I folded my arms. 'So, are you going to show me how you do it? How you unlock the doors?'

428 raised an eyebrow. 'I really don't fancy giving all my secrets away, if it's all the same to you.'

'Surely not.'

'Look, if you'll just glance away…'

'No.'

There came a distant slamming noise. And then another one. Echoing. Getting closer.

'And what would that be?' I asked.

428 gave me a look. 'It's your prison. You should know this. That's the sound of lots of doors.'

'Yes. But what's causing it? 428, you must know!'

'I'm dying to find out.'

'Well, I'd rather not.' As soon as I said it, I realised

what a coward I sounded like. Perhaps I was. 'Listen to me 428 – we're safe in here. The door's locked.'

'Really?' 428 seemed amused. 'Whatever it is, it's probably looking for us. And when whatever it is finds that this door is the only one still locked…'

'Ah. There must be some way to keep it out.'

428 ignored me for a moment, crouched over against the door. I repeated the question.

'That's what I'm trying to do.' He sounded like his teeth were clenched. 'And you won't like it. So, seriously, look away, sir.'

'Oh, come on, you've a hidden key, is that it?'

'Shut up. We're too late. Listen. It's coming…'

The slamming got closer and closer as door after door rattled and then bounded open. Then came three loud bangs against the door of our cell. And then… nothing.

'It knows we're in here, 428.' I whispered.

'Doctor, please,' said 428. 'At times like this it's nice to hear my name. Helps me think. Could you ask me some obvious questions too? That also helps.'

'All right… Doctor. It knows we're in here.'

'Yes. Tricky,' admitted 428. 'And there is literally no way I can keep it out.'

Three more bangs. Huge dents appeared in the cell door. The hinges started to buckle.

'How…' I was puzzled. 'How come the door won't open? The handle's on the other side.'

'Ah yes,' 428 stood up, looking a little sheepish. 'But the electron magnet is on this side.'

'What?'

He pointed to a small metal object on the door handle. 'I, ah, made it in the craft workshop.'

'You did what?'

'It's saving our lives now, isn't it? You're being a tad ungrateful.'

'How did you…'

Three more dents and a terrible tearing noise.

'Now, really?'

'I'd rather not die curious.'

428 gave me a strange look at that. 'Fine. I didn't eat the porridge for breakfast but I kept the spoon. They're iron. I then removed some wiring from a circuit breaker and the battery from an emergency light and a few other things and hey presto. The fiddly bit was jamming the lock just now. I had to reverse the polarity of… of my spoon.'

'Right.' I was a little impressed.

'I have done this before. Sort of.' 428 coughed. 'That's not the point. It won't hold up against that for long. What we need is another way out of here. Quickly. Any ideas?'

'No.'

'Just, you are the Governor. This is your prison.'

'It's trying to kill me at the moment.'

'Ask it not to?'

'Do you ever stop being like that?'

'Oh no, sometimes I'm positively breezy.' The Doctor leaned back against the cell wall. He looked as tired as I felt.

There came a loud wrenching sound and the door heaved slowly out of its socket, taking much of the asteroid wall with it. And for a few seconds something huge and terrible and all in shadow loomed over us and then…

I shut my eyes at that point. Not because I am a coward but because I was tired. I keep telling you. I was very tired that day. I'd slept lightly. Bad dreams.

The last thing I saw was 428 standing between me and whatever it was on the other side of that door. He looked defiant. Even though his back was to me, I knew he was staring at it.

And it went away.

As in, well, what really happened was that I closed my eyes, getting ready for death. Seeing my life. Everything I'd done wrong. Making my peace. Death did not come. I opened my eyes again. No sign of the creature. Just a shredded metal door rocking on the floor.

428 turned to me, and let out a delighted little puff of air.

'It went away… you stared at the monster and it went away?'

428 considered the idea and then dismissed it. 'I'm good, but I don't think I'm that good.'

'So, what was it?'

'Not a clue,' 428 grinned wickedly. 'Let's go and find out.'

We stepped out into the corridor. I was theorising out loud.

'There's some kind of alien creature hiding in this Prison? Perhaps it was… travelling on the asteroid?'

'OK,' 428 was picking his way gently along the darkened corridor. 'Good notion. Carry on with that.'

'Asleep… somewhere… throughout the building of the prison… and now it's woken up and it's hungry and we've given it a lot of food.'

'Kind of handy, don't you think? Oh, I'm sleepy, I'll just hide in some solid rock. Maybe breakfast will deliver itself. Bring me bacon.' 428 shook his head, running his hands through his hair.

'Clara's nice,' I said for something to say.

'Yes, yes she is.' 428 considered then pulled up in the corridor, looking alarmed. 'You've met her? What's she doing here?'

'Mounting a one-woman protest for your release on the landing pad. There are placards.'

'She'll win,' said 428, and, despite myself, I found myself nodding. We smiled. We smiled at each other. For a moment, I wondered if, despite everything, 428 was my friend.

Then we heard the crying. 428 noticed it first – he was already running towards it before I'd even cottoned on. In the shadows, something was moving. It was a figure in a wheelchair, crying.

I knew who it was even before I heard the voice.

'It doesn't like me,' the voice wailed. 'It came for all the others but it ran away from me.'

428 was crouched down by the pathetic figure. 'What did? What happened to you? Did it do this to you? Who are you?'

I spoke, my voice shaking. 'That, 428, is Prisoner 117. Marianne Globus.'

Marianne Globus was the first person to try and escape from the Prison. She made it to the landing pad. She didn't get further.

'That's all you're going to tell me?' 428 stared in horror at the creature crying to itself in the wheelchair. 'Those injuries…' Then he looked closer. 'Is that chair made out of…'

'We customised a Custodian,' I said and, absurdly, horridly, I giggled. 'Sorry,' I said. 'Sorry. Really.'

Prisoner 428 carried on glaring at me and I knew then how that monster must have felt.

'We had no choice,' I continued. 'Marianne… Her injuries were such…'

'What injuries? What exactly happened?'

Marianne looked up. When she spoke, her voice was a thin croak. That's all she had left. 'It got hot. Then it got cold.' She shuddered, her movement so restricted she simply flapped around in the chair.

I shook my head and talked softly, patting her hand. 'You did ever so well, Marianne,' I said gently.

'I escaped,' she said. 'Did I escape?'

'Yes, yes, of course. You're free now.'

'Am I?' The head moved around blindly and managed an awful smile. 'I guess I am. I like your voice. Are you my friend?'

'Of course I am,' I said softly. 'Always.'

'Good.' The head jerked at Prisoner 428. 'Beware of friends!' she snapped, suddenly alert and fierce. 'They betray you. They always let you down.'

Prisoner 428 stared at me. 'What happened?'

Marianne Globus was the first person to try and escape from the Prison. She made it to the landing pad. She didn't get further.

We made our way along the corridor, 428 pushing Marianne's chair. He didn't need to. It was gliding by itself. 428 was simply using it as a way of ignoring me. 'So, Marianne,' he said, 'the power to your chair is still working. But not to the lights or to the other Custodians.'

'Who are now missing,' I said.

'Shut up,' said 428.

'Don't tell me to—'

'Shut up,' 428 repeated.

We moved on slowly in silence.

Marianne started to sing a song. Her broken voice echoed along the empty corridor.

'Twinkle Twinkle, Little Star

How I wonder what you are

Up above the world so high…'

She paused, her voice having long ago left the notes behind.

'Like a diamond.' She giggled and then started to cry again. 428 patted her, smoothing down what remained of her hair, and she drifted off into sleep.

Marianne Globus was the first person to try and escape from the Prison. She made it to the landing pad. She didn't get further.

'Fine,' my voice was heavy. 'Prisoner 117 made it to the landing pad. She waited for a shuttle to come. We didn't notice she'd gone. When we don't turn the lights on, it gets very cold out there. There are two places to wait on the landing pad where you won't be seen on the cameras. She picked the wrong one. The one where the shuttle engines are vented when they come in to land.'

428 carried on stroking Marianne, who whimpered

in her sleep as though she was remembering.

'And…' My voice cracked, 'We didn't find her then. We didn't find her till a long time afterwards. After we'd turned off the lights and it had got cold. Very cold. We did what we could…'

We finished our circuit of Level 6. There were no prisoners. No Custodians. No monster. Just Marianne. Whatever it was had gone. We reached the lift. 428 held his spoon up. It made a noise.

'Pretty noise!' cooed Marianne in her slumber.

'Yes it is,' said 428. 'It's a sonic spoon. I'm going to use it to access this hatch and try and get some reserve power into the lift.' The hatch fell off, and 428 reached inside. With a shudder the lifts opened.

428 pushed Marianne into the lift.

'Are we going on a ride?' she asked.

'Yes,' he said. 'We're going to get you to a doctor.'

'A doctor?' she giggled. 'I like the sound of a doctor.'

'So do I,' agreed 428.

428 and Marianne stood in the lift. I paused on the threshold. Behind me, the empty Level 6 whispered to itself. The air felt foetid. A light flickered. Then another.

I wasn't invited, but I stepped into the lift anyway. The doors shut. We rode up.

'We did our best,' I said. 'But lying out there for so long in so much pain… We just… keep her… as sedated as we can.'

'You clearly do that.'

'He's my friend,' Marianne told 428 excitedly.

'Shut up!' I heard myself snap at her. 'I did my best for you, I really did.'

'Yes,' 428 murmured into where her ear should have been. 'Only some people's best really isn't very good, is it?'

We took the rest of the ride in silence.

The doors opened. Bentley was waiting with Guardians and Custodians.

'Governor!' she said with some surprise, 'You're all right. What happened?'

428 started to speak, but Bentley felled him with a blow and he sank down winded.

'I… I…' Funny when you sometimes hear your own voice and you think 'Do I really sound like that? How can people bear to hear that?' I could see people watching me. I was faltering, weak. I knew I mustn't show weakness – especially not in front of Bentley. I didn't deserve anyone's pity. Instead I pulled myself sharply together. The voice I heard myself speaking in now was a proper voice. A strong voice. A commanding voice. A Governor's voice.

'I reached Level 6. The power outages had opened all the doors. When I got there, I found 428 but no other prisoners. The only other witness or survivor is 117. I recommend she be placed in protective custody until she is well enough to speak. If necessary, withdraw pain medication if that helps her become lucid.'

I heard 428's breathless protest, but one of Bentley's guardians hit him again, so I continued.

'I saw something.' I made sure I didn't falter on this. 'There is something down there. It may be in league with 428. It may simply be a hologram or some such that he has…' I was aware of how ludicrous I sounded, but I pressed on, 'Something he has designed to confuse us. I believe 428 should be placed in an intense custody suite and interrogated. He may be involved in the power outages. He is our only suspect for the disappearance of the prisoners on Level 6.'

I could see him glaring at me with silent fury. I didn't acknowledge it. 'I'm going to file a report now,' I said, rubbing my eyes. 'I'll do it from my room. I don't want to oversee the interrogation – I'm tired, so very tired. Oh, and search 428. He has a spoon.'

7

The girl was there on the launch pad. I left her there.

The girl was back on the launch pad the next day. She'd brought along an ancient whiteboard, and she wrote on it in pen: 'I AM A VISITOR. AREN'T YOU OBLIGED TO SEE ME ONCE?'

'I don't know what she's playing at,' I said.

Bentley shrugged. 'She could write any form of sedition on that.'

'Is that a worry?' I asked.

'She is an associate of 428.' As if to prove it, Clara started to carve cabbalistic signs on the whiteboard. I would have dismissed it as nonsense only… what if this was some kind of coded computer virus, picked up and recoded by the cameras? Perhaps that was how the systems failures were being triggered. How 428's accomplices were receiving their instructions.

I went down to see her.

*

'There you are! Hello!' she beamed as I emerged onto the landing pad. She threw out her hand. It impacted with the electric field. She winced and snatched it back. 'You could have told me that was there.'

'You knew it was there, Clara,' I wasn't in the mood. 'What is the code that you are you drawing?'

'Noughts and crosses.' She tapped the board. 'Want to play?'

'Not an…' I started to form the sentence 'alien computer virus' in my head but it dwindled and slunk away. 'Never mind.'

'Are you the Governor here?' she asked.

'You know I am.'

'And you're supposed to call on someone the first time they visit, aren't you?'

'You've visited here three times already,' I was bored.

'Ohhhh,' she sighed. 'Excuse me,' she walked off round the corner. I heard her shouting and kicking something made out of wood. She came back. 'I'm sorry,' she said. 'Small argument with my transport.' She shrugged. 'Let's pretend I'm a time traveller.'

'No harder than pretending you are the Queen of Jordan.'

'I'm sorry?' She looked puzzled and then her face cleared. 'See, now, what I'm doing, is I am pretending I am a time traveller and that this is actually my first meeting with you in order to fool you into giving me a second meeting—'

'Fourth.'

'So guess what – it's worked!' She clapped. 'I'm delightful.'

'You're overdoing it,' I said.

'Just a little,' she admitted. 'On my bad days, Katy Perry wonders who's stolen all her twee.'

'Where's this going? I am rather busy.'

'So am I,' she said, 'I've got to fit in three previous meetings with you. And then there's my art class with 2B. Need to give them a project. No ideas, have you?'

'Placards,' I suggested. 'FREE THE DOCTOR'.

'You're kidding. Does it work?' she asked hopefully.

'Maybe,' I said.

'Well, I'll consider it,' she said seriously. 'Listen, can you do something for me? It's the Doctor's birthday—'

'Is it?'

'No, but let's pretend,' she beamed. 'And I've got him a present.'

'Prisoners aren't allowed presents.'

'But he's over two thousand years old. Well over. I think. Don't know how many more birthdays he'll have. Back in a jiff.' She went around the corner. The door to her unseen spacecraft opened with a wooden creak. She came back, holding an elaborately decorated cake. 'Ta da!' she said, placing it on a rock. 'It could be worse. I could have made cupcakes. That would have been unbearable. Also, I find cakes tricky, so I threw all my eggs in one mixing bowl and just did the one big cake.'

'The one big, not at all suspiciously big cake?'

'That's the one.'

'Anything hidden inside it?'

'Nu-huh.' She shook her head solemnly. 'Scout's honour. Not that I ever was a scout. But I have collected children from Scouts and listened to them talk about lighting fires. So I am practically a scout.'

'Back to the cake,' I said. 'You expect me to take this cake and present it to your friend?'

'Yes,' she said.

'Funny candle,' I said.

We both surveyed the cake.

'Ah,' she said. 'Well, he's, as I said, over two thousand, and that's quite the fire hazard in candles, so I just went for one big special candle.'

'It's metal and it glows.'

'I know!' she clapped her hands together. 'Isn't it pretty?'

I leaned close to the fence. 'Funny thing. Your friend had something very like that in his possession when he entered this prison.'

'Really?' She was all innocence.

'He also recently made himself a device that could open doors. And it made a sound very similar to the one that candle is making.'

'Did he?' Her eyes were wide with innocence. 'He's

very clever. What was it?'

'A spoon.'

'Wow, you're kidding, a spoon?' Clara giggled. 'Do we always have this much fun when I come and see you?'

'Pretty much. Sometimes.'

'Well that's something. Then I shall definitely come and do this loads,' she said. 'Just checking though – no chance you'll take the cake?'

'None whatsoever,'

'Fair enough,' Clara sighed. 'I'll just give it to Danny and tell him it's because he's been nice. He'll like that.'

I suddenly felt… jealousy… about this Danny.

She gave me a mock salute. 'Well then, I'd best be off. See you earlier. Give the Doctor my love. I'm very envious. It sounds like he's having a delightful time.'

Prisoner 428 had not been cooperative. The Prison does not use or condone torture. The Approved Protocols forbid anything like torture. They even prescribe the allotted Safe Stress Positions. We do not allow torture.

428 went for his mandated exercise period. I did not notice the way he limped slightly, held his arm, or how his face looked. I was only watching on the camera out of curiosity. He had not provided Bentley and her team with any valuable information. I'm not really sure I expected him to know anything more.

I watched him pacing the bare-walled enclosure of the Isolation Exercise Cell. It's an empty, blank square. The stone floor had ground itself to dust under the steady pacings of the occupants. 428 walked around it slowly and steadily, his left leg dragging slightly.

'Are you happy?' he said, seemingly to no one.

As her tranquillisers wore off, Marianne had roused from her stupor. But she had not been very helpful. Obviously, she hadn't seen anything. She said she had heard something. But all she said she'd heard was screaming. A lot of screaming. And then she'd started to cry. So we sedated her again. This time very strongly. There was some question about whether it would be a good idea to rouse her from it. Her condition had deteriorated. I held her hand as she went under and she squeezed it tightly at first, and then gradually let go, like she was slipping away.

'You're my friend,' she said weakly, and I felt so empty.

'You know, this is all a waste of everyone's time.'

428's voice woke me from my reverie. He wasn't looking at the camera, simply marking out the room, thinking aloud.

'The Governor knows I don't know what's happened to the people on Level 6. I'd love to help. I really would. Before it's too late. And, if you let me out of here I... No, doesn't matter,' There was bitterness in his voice. 'What I can tell you is that there's something very wrong in this prison. I heard systems failures mentioned. I've experienced them. They're getting a little worse every day, aren't they? Every day that I'm kept in here. That's not, by the way, a threat. I just know that the sooner you let me out of this, the sooner I can help you sort this out. And save lives. I'm very good at that.'

Outrageous. I shook my head, sickened by him. His records proved that he was quite the reverse. His records had said that. No one who came here was innocent. That he insisted on this heroic pretence was somehow even more disturbing. I know that Bentley had shown him the files of his crimes during interrogation and he'd just laughed. Laughed in her face. I found that chilling.

Prisoner 428 continued to pace the Exercise Cell. Then he leaned against a wall and sighed. A long sigh of defeat.

When he spoke again his voice was softer. 'I can't get out. She can't get in. Time's running out. I've got to save them.' And then he shut his eyes. He'd told me he didn't sleep, but suddenly 428 looked very tired indeed.

Which was when the walls peeled apart and the Custodians emerged from their docking stations. They were as silent as ever. Four of them. They converged on 428, who eyed them warily.

'Oh, so that's what this is, is it?' he said. He began to circle them, looking for an escape route. There was none. Their slim cylinders cracked open and antenna emerged. Sharp antenna.

My first instinct was a thrill of pleasure. Good, I thought. Let him suffer. Time to pay for all that you've done, 428.

The Custodians closed in on 428. One sliced at him and he fell back, a cut running down his cheek and his sleeve.

'So now we know,' 428 was grim, holding his arm, dodging around the Custodians. The Custodians closed in on 428. I could no longer see him, but I could hear his cries.

'Now we know the kind of Governor you really are. You're not worth saving after all.'

That was unfair. I shouted in my office where no one heard me. This wasn't quite what I'd been expecting. I was on my feet, blipping the Control Station. I had to stop this. No one was answering my blip. No one at all.

On screen, the Custodians closed in on 428 again.

I ran out into the Control Station. Everyone there declared they knew nothing about what was going on. A shade truculently. I ordered the Custodians in the Exercise Cell deactivated, but they did not respond to the command circuit. Or, the people on duty told me they did not.

I ran down to the Exercise Cell. The Governor has an override. I can open almost every door inside the Prison. This had gone too far. This prison does not allow torture or violent punishment.

I knew Bentley was following me. She was shouting. Bentley should not shout at me. I could hear cries coming from the cell. It would open to my palm print.

Only it didn't. The alert signal went off.

We were caught in a power outage.

Bentley glowed with satisfaction. '428 comes under attack and a power outage happens. Most convenient. That proves a theory of mine.'

'Did you – did you authorise this? What's going on in there?' I demanded, shouting, full of fury.

Bentley looked dead ahead, voice cold. 'I had no idea, Governor.'

'I don't believe you,' I said. 'Open that door.'

Bentley produced a manual key. It would take time. But we still had over six minutes.

Inside the Exercise Cell all was silent. I was expecting to see the battered body of 428. I think that was all I was supposed to have found. I wasn't supposed to have been watching. The camera footage would have been mysteriously corrupted and all that we would have had to go on was 428's broken body.

But there was no body. Just four deactivated

Custodians. Four very damaged Custodians.

Had 428 done it again? Had he tricked us and escaped?

The seal to a docking station opened, and 428 staggered out. He was in a mess, but he was alive.

'So,' he grinned. 'Hard luck. I'm still alive. I couldn't open the door, but I could get into the docking station. Nice place to be while those four knocked seven bells out of each other.'

'It was… I had no idea… It wasn't supposed to happen.'

'Clearly the systems outage affected their programming' said Bentley, coldly. 'An accident.'

428 held up a hand, bored by us. He yawned.

A new alarm sounded. The power outage had become an Imminent Systems Failure.

'Right then, tickety-boo,' growled 428. 'Another power outage? Let's go and have a look, shall we?'

428 stood in the Control Station. He moved swiftly from panel to panel, warily ducking under and around Custodians. By the time we got there, the systems failure was at over a minute.

'I'm guessing that at about seven minutes things start to go critical and you have to phase out various systems.'

I was impressed he'd got that.

Bentley wasn't. 'You worked that out suspiciously

quickly.'

428 nodded. 'I did, didn't I?' He clearly didn't care what she thought.

I could sense the tension between the two of them. In an ideal world I'd have him back in solitary by now and Bentley under close supervision pending an investigation. But there wasn't time.

This time we were totally locked out.

428 stepped back. Clearly he'd completed his survey of the Control Station.

'Bentley was right for once,' he said. 'Nothing's responding. I'm wondering if there's a way to delay things – buy a little more time.'

'Only if we eject Level 7,' I told him.

'What is Level 7?'

'I don't like to talk about it,' I admitted. I was aware of Bentley watching me. I knew that whatever I said now would be brought up later. I never could say the right thing in front of her.

'Clearly you don't want to talk about it, Governor. But you're in a lot of trouble.'

'Level 7 is a self-contained unit of the prison. It is a large storage crate.'

'I see. And what's it doing here?'

'Storage.'

'Of what?'

I felt uncomfortable. 'My job... my job is the safe

running of the Prison. Mostly, Level 7 falls outside of my jurisdiction.'

'But you know what it is?'

'It's outside my remit.'

'You know,' 428 tapped his teeth with his fingers, 'after the Second World War the villagers near Dachau claimed not to know about the death camp on their doorstep. Not a clue. Utter innocence. Wide eyes. An American general couldn't quite believe it. And yet he almost did. The village was so near the death camp, but seemed so utterly normal, so quiet, innocent. Until he realised no one in the village hung their washing outside to dry. Because of the smell.'

'What are you saying?'

'Level 7 stinks. And you know it does.'

'It's not my responsibility.'

428 made a disgusted noise. 'And you were only obeying Protocols.' He glared at me.

'I'll blip the commander of Level 7. We call him the Oracle.'

I called up the Oracle on my tablet. He stared out of the screen, his fat eyes filled with delight, his fingers waggling in excitement at seeing me.

'Ah! Why, it is you, Governor, and I knew it would be. And who can this be…? Why yes, of course, this is Prisoner! 4! 2! 8! How wonderful. I wish I could say unexpected, but I knew it would be so, I shall, yes I must, settle for Wonderful.'

428, for once, was lost for words. He glanced at me. 'What's his deal?'

The Oracle was still at 'Wonderful to see you, 428. How can I help?' He tapped his fingers on the screen, a pit-a-pat of oily raindrops.

428 looked about to ask a lot of questions. I cut across. 428 was many things, but useless at diplomacy. The Oracle required careful handling. Otherwise, well, his charges had been rumoured to suffer. 'Oracle,' I said. 'The latest power drain is critical. The station is reaching, ah, cascade failure. We're going to eject you so that you can launch a beacon. So that you... your charges may stand some chance.'

The Oracle beamed and rubbed his fingers slowly across each other. 'Oh, yes, why yes, I shall tell the children. They will be pleased! A trip! Everyone does so love an outing.' He frowned, and his piggy eyes squinted till they were little glitters of coal. 'But the weather will be bad. I know that, sadly.' He wagged a finger disapprovingly. 'I'm seeing lots of mauve.'

'Children?' muttered 428 ominously.

I nodded.

'You keep children in prison?'

The Oracle looked up sharply. 'I told you he wouldn't be happy. And he doesn't like me already. A man of taste and discrimination! Ha ha.' He leaned into the tablet, filling the screen with his smile and his hands. 'Why yes, Prisoner 428. My little crate is rammed to the rafters with the families of dissidents. People on HomeWorld who are perhaps a little out of favour… but not out-of-favour enough to be shipped here. The kind of lovely, loyal people who will be extra lovely and loyal knowing that their children are hostages. My cargo is most, most precious… and, as I said, will just adore an outing.' He clapped his hands together and giggled.

It was a repellent display and it wasn't wasted on 428.

'Ejecting Level 7 is a great idea. Get them out of here,' he said. He turned back to me. 'This isn't over.'

I noticed that 428 was behaving like he was in charge again. I didn't care for that.

I nearly said 'Do as he says,' but knew that Bentley would object. Instead, I called up the schematic and activated the ejection procedure myself.

The Custodians quivered. Bentley assented with a grunt, and they hurried into action Level 7 was launched.

Level 7 was launched.

The Oracle's face appeared on the screen. 'Oh dear. How magnolia. Didn't I tell you there'd be bad weather? We're not moving.'

Bentley scanned the display panel. 'There's not enough energy left in the system to operate the automatic eject.'

'But…' The Oracle grinned. 'I've got engines. Can't I

just fire up my toasty little "Baxter Drive"?' He put the quotes round the name himself and I really wished he hadn't.

'Not with the clamps engaged,' I told him. 'You'd just tear Level 7 in half.'

'Ah, I hadn't foreseen that,' The Oracle ran his fingers down his nose. 'But I just know you'll come up with something else clever. An even better idea. Just in the nick of time.' He leaned back in his chair and smiled. Waiting.

'I already have come up with something.' 428 was running for the door. 'I'm going to release the clamps on manual.'

A Custodian blocked his exit.

'Get this thing out of my way,' 428 snapped.

'He is a prisoner, sir.' Bentley was moving over swiftly, her soft voice almost lost in the constant blare of the alarms. She was making it easy for me. Do nothing. Obey Protocols. Let it go. We tried. It didn't work. Never mind. We'd all go down together. No one could blame us.

This time 428 hadn't even fully turned around before I spoke.

'Custodian, stand down. Prisoner 428 is engaged in Governor Authorised Work Duty.' The Custodian hesitated. I wasn't used to this. 'I repeat, this has Governor Authorisation. Let him pass. No, in fact, go with him, assist him.'

The Custodian processed this and moved to one side, springing some antennae that were, I'm sure, supposed to be helpful but looked rather formidable.

'Ah, splendid,' 428 eyed them warily, 'I'd rather go alone if it's all the same to you.'

I could have gone back to my office to watch, but I remained in the Control Station, watching on the large screen along with everyone else. We could track 428 racing from camera to camera, hurtling his way down through the Prison. Someone had put an overlay up to show how much time had elapsed. As he ran, 428 was yelling. He clearly had excellent lung capacity, or was used to giving orders while running at high speed.

'This is not an order. I know you don't like them. So this is a request. I'm going to do what I can to release Level 7. I would like you to consider... just consider, mind... putting as many of the Prisoners as you can onto Level 7 before it leaves. We are turning it into a life raft. I do think, don't you, that no matter what people have done, they deserve a chance. But it's just a suggestion. Barely more than a hint.'

He stopped in his pell-mell scramble, ducking into a workshop where he grabbed some breath, a wrench and a blowtorch.

'I need these,' he said, not even turning to the camera as he rifled through drawers, stuffing things into his pockets. 'Can you release the security coding on any objects I remove from the workshop? Don't want the system setting off lots of alarms and keeping me hanging around waiting like a shoplifting granny, do we?' He turned, and his smile was all charm.

Bentley looked at me. I nodded. The security barriers at the door to the workshop deactivated.

'Splendid,' said 428, grabbing a trolley. 'In that case, I've always wanted to win a supermarket sweep,' And he was off, running with an anti-grav trolley hastily crammed full of tools banging down the stairs.

He made it in a minute and a half. Other cameras showed Bentley's Guardians herding Prisoners into Level 7. I had expected more of a discussion (at some volume) about this.

'I think it's the right thing to do,' I had said.

'Is that your order, Governor?' Bentley had asked. I tried to work out her tone, but it was flat. Carefully flat.

I'd nodded. 'And as many Guardians, of course, as wish to go.'

Bentley had coughed. 'I believe I speak for us all when I say that we would prefer to stay. To try and resolve this situation and to tend for those Prisoners unable to board Level 7.'

'That's very noble of you,' I said to Bentley. 'But, obviously, if any Guardians feel that… Well, it's open to you all.'

There were nods, but no one looked at me. I think they were all deciding whether they wanted to live or die. And that should always be a private decision.

A camera finally found Prisoner 428. His wiry figure was squeezed into a service shaft (I dreaded to think how he'd got into it), wrapping itself around various pipes. He reached four mounds in the duct floor, spaced out between various vents and grilles.

'If I've memorised your schematic, this is where the release clamps are. Wondered what these beauties were.' He tapped four objects, which, now I looked at them, did seem remarkably like clamps. 'And yes, the power has failed to them. Still, not a problem.' He wielded a lever. 'Archimedes once said to me that if I gave him a lever big enough, he could move the world,' He threw the lever over his shoulder. 'Sadly, not going to work this time.'

He sank to the floor, regarding the clamps like a chess master, then pulled out the blowtorch. 'I need to soften the metal up a bit, and this thing should be pretty effective.'

He got to work, playing flames from the torch's highest setting over the metal. I could tell it was pretty hot, as the surrounding cladding on various pipes began to smoulder, filling the screen with smoke.

428 worked in silence apart from the occasional

cough. Then he stood up and reached for the lever, 'Kind of like making a crème brûlée. Chat about cooking with Clara won't you, eh, next time you see her?'

He was talking to me.

'It's just…' He began working his lever under one of the clamps, and, true to his word, it did start to twist like spun sugar. 'I rather fear the conversation you have with her will be a bit glum otherwise, ooh, there we go. That's one.' He moved on to the next clamp. 'Tell your weird Oracle to behave himself and get the Baxter Drive ready. Which, incidentally, I'm standing on top of. That's what all the grilles are for. In case you were curious. I assure you I'm very curious about them. I'm basically stood on top of a giant radioactive pressure cooker. Ah-ha, two down.' 428 leant back, staggering a little. 'The Greek God Vulcan did all his best metalwork at the bottom of a volcano. I tell you now, Health and Safety would be on him like a ton of bricks. Yeah… already getting a little toasty.' The picture was swimming slightly and the smoke was everywhere in the duct.

428 started on the third clamp. 'I can tell he's started up the drive. I hope your Oracle's a poppet and doesn't fully engage until I've finished. It really would be awful being poached for nothing.'

Hearing this, Bentley began a frantic conversation. I could see the access door to Level 7 was now shut.

I could also see that power levels across the prison were sinking dangerously low. The air was becoming stifling. My throat tickled. I was beginning to feel sympathy with 428's terrible situation.

'Here's the thing,' said 428, 'You can see it's not very likely I'm coming out of here alive. You've worked that out. I'm a clever man. So I can – ah, left the blowtorch burning, which isn't helping but not much can be done about that now – doesn't matter, not when about 20 seconds after this clamp is released this whole corridor is going to flood with Baxter Drive exhaust. And, at 20.000001 seconds there'll be nothing left of me. Even the prison food won't survive that. So there we go.'

I knew what he was doing. He was going to sacrifice himself to save everyone on board Level 7. To make up for – no, to go some way to make up for – all those he'd killed.

Clamp three perished. As it did so a new alarm started sounding.

'Hmm, fire alarm, how ironic,' chuckled 428. 'Anyway, consider this my last request. Really, think hard about who you're working for. Doesn't matter if you try and do good. Are *They* doing good?' The last clamp surrendered, and 428 sank onto the ground, exhausted, choking on the air.

'You're clear. Not long left. Tell the Oracle to go.'

Bentley did. I could feel the station judder as the

Baxter Drive engaged. Normally our anti-gravs would have compensated slightly, but they'd clearly given up.

428 sat on the floor, breathing shallowly. He gave me a wave. I could just see it through the fumes clogging the duct.

'Anyway,' his exhausted voice rattled, 'I guess you could consider this my last escape, Governor.'

'Yes,' I smiled. 'Thank you, Doctor.'

He nodded.

The screen was filled with smoke and flame. Alarms shrilled and wailed.

The asteroid jumped again as Level 7 kicked away from us explosively. There was a small bang followed by a bigger one. Everyone was watching Level 7 drift away from the station on the monitors. Well, everyone except me – I kept watching 428's face, serene, right up until the camera flared up red and then went black.

Then, ashen, but with little better to do, I watched what everyone else was watching. Level 7 powering away from the Prison. It only had a Baxter Drive, probably not enough to get it to a colony, or even to within rescue distance of a colony, but at least everyone on there stood a chance.

Which was more than could be said for us. After some cheering, I could sense the initial elation fading away. Systems failure. We all realised we were the ones left behind, stuck on a dying, crippled rock.

If only, I thought, if only 428 had been alive, whatever kind of man he'd been, he would have known what to do.

We all watched Level 7 turn and increase speed, travelling beyond the TransNet communications ring, beyond the artificial gravity gimbal, and towards the Defence Array, built to keep intruders out. It was a symbolic farewell. As Level 7 passed slowly through them, it really sank home to me that they were leaving us behind.

I was going to die on this rock. But at least we'd done it. We'd given them a chance.

Which was when the Defence Array powered up and blasted Level 7 into dust.

8

It was odd to be in one of my own cells.

I had visited many, talked with inmates in them, supervised them to make sure they were correctly kitted out. But I had never dreamed that I would actually be held in one.

It was very small. The bunk was just too short and too hard to be comfortable. The blanket was a tiny bit shorter and thinner than would have been adequate, and the pillow little more than a cardboard cut-out of one.

Everything in the cell lacked colour. Each object, if you picked it up and examined it, had a colour. Just about. But put together it achieved little more than a nullity.

The only thing of any colour was my orange uniform. And even then, the shade was somehow dirty and insipid. It merely served to mark me out as guilty.

And I felt guilty.

*

We stood watching Level 7 explode. It took a long time.

Someone cried out in shock. Later, watching the recordings, I realised it was me – the first voice on the recordings... Actually, here it is:

Bentley: *Governor.*

ME: *Yes?*

Bentley: *Gov – Sorry – Governor. Sir. I must, formally...*

ME: *Yes. You'd better. I think you had.*

Bentley: *Governor, I must formally place you under arrest. You will be investigated over... over the...*

ME: *Massacre. I think that's the right word you're looking for, isn't it?*

Bentley: *Over the deaths of those on board Level 7.*

ME: *Yes. Yes. I'm sorry. I'm sorry. What have I done? It's all my fault.*

Bentley: *Governor, it is my duty to advise you that logged recordings of all...*

ME: *I know. I know. I'm sorry. Can I sit down?*

Bentley: *I am afraid not, Governor. Would you like me to arrange for counsel for you?*

ME: *You had probably better stop calling me Governor.*

Bentley: *Very well, sir. Custodian, remove the Accused to a holding cell. We... we have a lot of vacant ones now.*

*

The cell bore no indication of recent habitation. It had been thoroughly cleaned by a Custodian. But that was little consolation. The previous inhabitant's desperation and hopelessness hung around it, filled what little space there was. There really wasn't that much room left for my own despair.

Occasionally a Custodian would come and remove me for an interview. I lost track of how much time had passed. Had I been in there a few minutes or days? It seemed so meaningless. I noticed the lights were dimmer, the air more stifling. I asked if they'd managed to recover the systems, but no one answered me. No one acknowledged me at all. But then, I was no longer Governor.

Lafcardio was one of the prisoners who'd stayed behind. He'd been head of the Law Faculty at a University. I asked for him to be my lawyer. He was shown into my interview cell. His voice was still husky from the fire in his library. He'd come from sickbay.

By law recordings between accused and counsel are privileged and not to be recorded. Here is the transcript:

ME: *Thank you for coming, Lafcardio.*
Lafcardio: 327, please, Governor.
ME: *I'm not the Governor any more.*

Lafcardio: No. I know that.

ME: You can use my real name. It's been so long since I've heard it.

Lafcardio: It is all right, sir.

ME: You know what I am accused of?

Lafcardio: Of being somehow responsible for the destruction of Level 7 with the loss of life of all those aboard.

ME: It's awful It's… I mean, having thought about it… 428, it was his idea…

Lafcardio: Are you seeking to make 428 responsible for what happened?

ME: No, no, of course not. It's just… Anyway, I'm sorry. I'm so sorry for what happened. But I was just trying my best. You can see that, can't you?

Lafcardio: I can see that that's what you believe.

ME: We've got to get this resolved, you and I. Between us, eh? The station is crippled. But 428 was right. There's something else going on here. It's absolutely correct that Bentley should ask me to step aside while this is resolved, but we need to do that immediately so that I can put my strength behind finding out what's going on here.

Lafcardio: I see. You want to resume being Governor after what's happened? You think that's what's right?

ME: Well, I mean, ideally, no. But The Prison needs a Governor. More now than ever.

Lafcardio: And that should be you?

ME: *Well… yes. Yes. Which is why I need you as my counsel. You can help. Can't you?*

Lafcardio: I am afraid, sir, I must decline.

ME: *What?*

Lafcardio: I must decline.

ME: *But surely… you can see. I mean, it was all an accident. I wasn't to blame. I'm not guilty. I need you.*

Lafcardio: So you say.

ME: *But surely… surely Lafcardio –*

Lafcardio: 327, please.

ME: *All right, dammit, 327. Surely, 327, we are friends. Aren't we?*

Lafcardio: Friends?

ME: *YES!*

Lafcardio: I would define the Doctor as my friend. I wish you good day.

ME: *Lafcardio!*

[Lafcardio stands up.]

ME: *I'm sorry for everything. And I'm sorry about your books.*

[Lafcardio leaves.]

I don't know how much later the hearing was. Possibly only a few minutes. It was fairly straightforward. Bentley sat opposite me with two more Guardians flanking her, and two Custodians behind me. Up close, I realised how intimidatingly blank they were. When they produced an antenna, you had no idea if it was to restrain or blast, to feed or inject. Whenever one came close, I instinctively flinched.

Bentley read everything out. All the charges.

How I had overridden Protocol, allowing 428 to place Level 7 in jeopardy. How I had allowed him to steal prison property in order to sabotage the safety retainers of Level 7. How I had given instructions that Level 7 was to be loaded with prisoners, and then ordered it to fly past the Defence Array.

It was useless to protest that the Defence Array had malfunctioned, that it wasn't supposed to fire on the ship. It was put to me that the whole prison had suffered a cascade failure and that, as such, direct control over the Defence Array could not be anticipated. I was asked if I had even checked what the status of the Defence Array was. I had not. Of course I had not. In the excitement of thinking I'd saved some lives, of course I had not.

'There wasn't time,' I heard myself saying. 'I mean, if I'd known, of course I would have.'

Bentley had looked me in the eye then. For the first time ever. 'There were 300 people on board Level 7 along with a further 235 prisoners.'

'I know,' I said. 'And I am sorry. But listen, can't we just…'

Nothing. I mean, a whole lot more was said, but nothing of interest.

*

I went and sat back in my cell. It felt utterly helpless. The air already had a stale, unpleasant taste to it. But maybe that was just me. I can't believe that, after all I'd just done, I sank into self-pity, but I did. I blamed 428. It had all been his idea. I had simply been following orders. That was all. Surely they'd see it. At any moment, and then they'd surely release me?

I wondered if I should pen a justification of my actions, and account for them. I began work on it. Putting to one side the horrific crimes of 428, you had to admit that the man was very persuasive. It was easy to fall into line with what he wanted. I suddenly saw, sharply and horribly, that I had become another of his victims. Is this what he'd been planning all along? To use me as a tool in order to kill off the people on the ship?

What had he said? 'Give me a big enough lever and I can move the world.' That was it. That was all I had been to him. A lever to allow him to pull off one last, audacious slaughter. I had been made a fool of and used, but I had been genuinely acting from the best of intentions. His last victim.

My account also brought the Oracle, HomeWorld and Bentley in for a fair amount of criticism, but it really was the Doctor who bore the brunt of it. What, I thought, I wouldn't give for another chance to see him.

It was a pretty pathetic document. I re-read it and

felt sick at myself. It was the kind of thing a coward would write. One who wouldn't take responsibility for his own mistakes.

I read it again, and actually, it didn't seem so bad.

But still, the fact remained, the one person who could help me out of all this was the one person who couldn't. Because the Doctor… because 428 was dead.

The door to my cell swung open. Standing there was the Doctor.

'Oh,' I said.

To my astonishment I started crying.

'"Hello" normally does just fine.' The Doctor looked embarrassed.

Obviously, I did a reasonable amount of inarticulate babbling. The Doctor didn't have much time for that.

'Listen, Governor,' he said. 'I'm springing you out of your own prison. If you want to actually enjoy the irony of that, I suggest you follow me sharpish.'

'Where to?' I asked.

'The last place anyone will think of looking for you,' smiled 428. 'My old cell.'

We got there, I later learned, because much of the CCTV had gone permanently off-line in the cascade failure. The system was keeping nearly all it could to itself to keep life support and gravity just about going. Even most of the Custodians had simply slid to a halt. Their Docking Stations still seemed to be working, but the power-up cycle refused to release them.

This meant that the remaining prisoners were having to be looked after by the human Guardians. Who were also rushed off their feet trying to hack back into the Prison systems.

Basically, the current regime was pretty lax. I made a note of all the various failings, should I need to counter-accuse Bentley of anything. 'You could get away with murder here,' I said.

'Probably not the best thing to say in a prison, you know,' answered 428, sliding the door of his cell open with a pretty nifty skeleton key.

'Where did you get that from?' I asked.

428 shrugged. 'You said I could take what I want from the workshop. Well, I did. I've been busy.'

'How long... how many days have I been in custody?'

'About four hours,' said 428. He shut the door of his cell behind us, and indicated we sit down on the bunk.

He plonked himself next to me. I flinched a little. Was I still afraid of him? Disgusted by him? Or somehow, despite everything, terribly pleased to see him?

'So,' said 428. 'Let's deal first of all with the good

news. Which is my remarkable escape.'

'Had you planned it?'

'No. Well, not exactly. But if Clara asks, do say yes. I'm just quite a quick thinker. Especially when I'm running. Exercise really sharpens the synapses. You see, I went into that tunnel knowing that I was basically going into the exhaust duct for Level 7's Baxter Drive. It all had to go somewhere. Now, then, you'll remember I took that blowtorch with me? Well, once I'd used it to soften up the clamps, I left it running.'

'Starting that small fire and all that smoke? Hardly a clever move.'

'You think not?' 428 arched an eyebrow. 'On the contrary, it was very clever. It's a powerful blowtorch. I turned it down to a lower setting so that anything flammable would smoulder and smoke, not burn. I needed smoke.'

'Why?'

'For the fire alarm. Remember it sounding? Well, I'd remembered what Bentley had said, that there was an ordinary fire alarm. And then there was the Flashpoint alarm, which went off thirty seconds prior to the section being sealed and the air from it being vented. I triggered the Flashpoint alarm. I'd done the maths in my head. If I could get myself vented far enough into space first then I wouldn't be poached, fried and scrambled by the Baxter Drive.'

'Oh.'

'Good, isn't it?'

'Well, wouldn't you still be in space?'

'A little. But there's an air-shell around the asteroid. Not much of one, I grant you, but enough of a safety net. And also, on my admittedly hurried way out, I did grab the blowtorch.'

'Did you?'

'All right then, fine, I'll admit, none of us had much of a choice. I ended up floating in space with all the tools I'd grabbed and that silly anti-grav trolley – which turns out not to be so silly when you're floating in space. Since tools are useful, I loaded as many of them as I could onto the trolley, and then fastened the blowtorch to the back of it. I turned the setting of it up to… 11. And then I escaped back into your prison.'

'What?'

'The Level 7 loading bay doors. Actually quite the weak spot. You should make a note of that. I just flew my trolley up to them and then used the blowtorch.'

'Can I just stop you. You broke into my prison on a flying trolley?'

428 grinned. 'Why not? I've escaped from it enough times using just a spoon.'

I hit him.

He looked surprised. 'That was… Well, that was ungrateful.'

'A lot of people have died,' I said.

'Yes… about that.' 428 stared at me. 'Didn't you think that was odd? The Defence Array firing like that?'

'Well, yes. But—'

'It wasn't doing what it was supposed to.'

'No.'

'And the Oracle didn't predict it. Funny, that.'

'No. Not funny. Not funny at all. You can't carry on running around like the world is just a grim joke to somehow laugh at. You've got to…'

'What have I got to do?' 428 rubbed his jaw, tired again. 'I really don't think you get to tell me how to behave any more, Governor. You've lost control of your Prison. Admit it. The Defence Array should have told you the game's up.'

'What do you mean?'

428 shook his head. 'You'll see in a bit. I'm very much afraid you will. But listen, just for the moment, let's stop thinking about the children, let's put the destruction of Level 7 to one side, shall we?'

'Why?'

'Because it'll stop you thinking clearly. I don't know about you, but it's pretty much all even my head can think about, and that's not helpful, is it?'

'No,' I said. I couldn't. Not for a moment. I would never.

428 tapped me on the forehead and my thoughts cleared.

'Good,' said 428. 'So, we're going to find out what's really going on here. And I think that'll tell you why the Defence Array blew up Level 7.'

The Prison seemed eerily deserted.

'Well, that's wrong,' I said. 'There should be about a hundred prisoners remaining.'

428 nodded. 'And we need to find them. Is Lafcardio still here?'

'Yes. But he's not talking to me.'

'Ah.' 428 smiled. 'But he will to me.'

We found the old man carrying some tattered books. 'When the prisoners fled, they left them behind,' he muttered, almost to himself. 'I knew they needed looking after. I just thought I'd collect them up and take them to the library. I was thinking of starting up again.'

'But this place is finished,' I did not say. 'OK.' That's what I said. I noticed Lafcardio wasn't looking at me. He was barely looking at 428. He was barely looking at anything.

'Who is left?' 428 asked him.

Lafcardio turned, focused with difficulty, and beamed at him, smiling. 'Delighted, genuinely delighted.' He pumped 428's hand enthusiastically.

428 detached himself and took one of the books from Lafcardio. He leafed through it. *The Barber of*

Seville? It really is funny what survives down through history, don't you think?'

Lafcardio nodded, seriously. 'There was a time, less than a millennium ago when it was still possible to have read every important book and most of the trivial ones. To quote from and discuss intelligently all of them. Now, oh now…' He laughed. 'It's not possible. It just isn't. One of the things I've liked about this place. So few books. Actually a blessing. It's made knowledge a finite thing. We had fewer than five thousand books. That's about half a dozen each at a time. But it's an easy sum for anyone to work through… Why, for the first time in my life, I found I actually had something in common with people from the Southern Worlds. If you'd asked me that a few years ago, I'd have laughed. But it turns out, no matter what colony you're from, you're in broad agreement that *Not a Penny More, Not a Penny Less* is Jeffrey Archer's best work.' He beamed at us both. 'And the classics! Why, the most surprising people spent their nights reading *The Arabian Nights* and dreaming of escape on a flying carpet.'

'I've flown on a carpet,' said 428, seemingly serious. 'It had fleas. And was worryingly saggy.'

Lafcardio smiled tolerantly. 'Of course you have. We used to have a copy of *The Phoenix and the Carpet*.' He looked suddenly crestfallen. 'It's gone now.'

We walked slowly along the corridors towards

where the library had once been. Devoid of people, The Prison still made noises to itself. Ghost doors slammed. Metal walkways ticked away like clocks. And it was getting warmer. Stiflingly so.

Even 428 had noticed. 'The air is getting stale. Oxygen content is becoming depleted already. The air units need to start recycling pretty soon.'

'Oh, I shouldn't worry,' Lafcardio muttered. 'They always sort it out here. The Governor is efficient to a fault.' He addressed this last remark to me, seemingly without realising I used to be the Governor. 'Ah, here we are.'

The Library was a mess. Many of the shelves had gone to make canteen furniture, but a few still remained, stretching away into the shadows of the room. Huge piles of unknowable junk, charred remnants of the venting, were cluttered around grilles. Even though the air had been emptied and recycled several times, the whole place still reeked, a sickly rich smell of burnt plastic.

Lafcardio placed his little handful of books on a shelf. They looked pathetic. 'Well,' he said, 'It's a start, isn't it? Every man has to start somewhere. And I'll get there.'

He pottered off among the debris, pulling out the occasional singed fragment of a book, sometimes little more than a spine and burnt margins, placing it hopefully on a shelf.

Soon he forgot we were even there, moving around, muttering to himself.

'We'll get you some more books,' I offered.

428 nodded. It was the right thing to say.

'Oh good.' Lafcardio rubbed his hands, then went back to plunging through the teetering stacks of debris. 'Something's glinting in here… All that glitters…'

We left him alone.

'The poor man's gone mad. He really wasn't much help,' I said to 428.

He gave me one of his chilling looks. 'Really? Did it not tell you that sometimes, somehow, life finds a way of continuing, of pressing on? Even if it has to blinker itself to a few unfortunate details of reality.'

'He needs help,' I said.

'No, no.' 428 smiled. 'I think you'll find he's the happiest person in here.'

Which was when we heard Lafcardio's scream.

We raced back through to the Library without even thinking of the danger we were in.

In a corner of the room lay the little old man's body, broken.

Looking around, the darkness loomed over us, huge and sinister. The piles of debris, the empty shelves, everything threw ominous shadows.

'Something in here killed him,' I said.

428 crouched over his body. 'Yes,' he said sadly. 'He was reading.' He tapped the open book still clutched in the man's hand. 'The Magician's Nephew. That's a good one.' He closed the book gently, laid it to rest on Lafcardio's chest, and then straightened slowly up. 'We should go.'

'Really?'

428's voice was very low. 'The door is just there. We should go.'

'But why?'

'Can you never whisper?' 428 hissed, 'Because the door is there and nothing came out of this room so…'

'What killed him is still in here?' I gasped.

'Oh, so you can whisper.' 428 nodded curtly.

We didn't make it for the door before it came for us. One of the piles of debris shifted and something rushed out of it at us. It was hard to see exactly what it was, what form it took, but it was swift and deadly.

It went for 428, or, rather, 428 went for it with a chair. All I could really see was him moving among shadows, crying out occasionally.

I made for the door.

I stood on the outside, pausing, trying to work out what to do next. I could seal the door. That was probably the safest thing. It would mean losing 428, but it would also mean I had trapped that creature – something else that may, just, have caused the problems I was accused of. Evidence. I tapped in the code to seal the door. It didn't work. They'd changed my passcode.

428 shot out. 'Ah, you waited for me? Brilliant!' He beamed at me. I noticed the jagged tears in his prison uniform. He was holding the battered remains of a chair. He tossed it back inside, and then pulled a spoon from his pocket. 'I made another one,' he laughed. With a whirr of noise, the door to the library sealed.

'What was that?' I asked.

'Frightening,' he replied. His smile had faded from his face. 'I've still no idea what it is, but it's lethal. It also appears to just kill.'

'How so?'

'It's no longer as curious. Nor is it cautious any more.'

'Any more?'

'It's the same thing we encountered on Level 6. It had been taking pains to cover up its tracks. Now it left Lafcardio's body for us to find. Either because it didn't care, or because he didn't have what it wanted, or it was luring us to…' His smile was grim, 'It's certainly clever.' He tapped his teeth with his fingers, 'It's a trap… in a trap.'

'What?' I said.

'I think that'll become apparent. We should go.'

'Too late,' said Bentley.

She was standing behind us, with a squadron of Guardians. They looked tired but very, very angry.

'Ah, hello,' said 428. 'You shouldn't have found us yet.'

'No,' agreed Bentley. 'But the Governor just used his pincode on the library door.'

'Oh. Oh, I see.' 428 gave me a look. I didn't see what it was, as I was staring at the floor. I took some comfort from the fact that Bentley had still called me Governor.

428 strode into the space between us and Bentley's Guardians.

'Now then, the problem is that I wanted to lay out a theory to you. A careful theory which convinced all of you, Prisoners and Guardians, to work together if you wanted to live.'

'I don't have any more time for your clever, lethal theories,' snapped Bentley. She stepped forward, and 428 swept up a hand.

'Neither do I,' he snapped. 'I needed to gather evidence. Build a convincing case. Avoid you finding us with any dead bodies. I've a procedure. It's tried and tested. Still,' he sighed, 'sometimes you improvise.'

428 held up his spoon.

Before any of the Guardians could draw and fire, the door to the library had sprung open and the thing was upon us all.

'What is that?' yelled Bentley.

'Later,' snapped 428. 'Just shoot it.'

The thing? I suppose I should describe the thing as it appeared. It was a fast-moving mass, taller than a man, and wider. At first it seemed to be wearing shadows, and then a cloak, and then I realised... It was covered in scraps of black plastic sheeting from the debris in the library. The tatters fluttered around it like streamers, disguising its true shape. Something glinted underneath. But I also had the strangest memory of childhood – seeing an ancient pantomime enacted. One where a dragon rushed across the stage. The dragon was a terrifying spectacle (especially when you were a 6-year-old boy), but even I could see that as it moved and twisted, the costume shifted and the joins revealed tiny hints of the operators inside – bits of an arm or a flank. It was the same here. Inside all that black sheeting was metal, but also what seemed to be a person.

It made a horrifying spectacle as it bore down on us. On the Guardians. On all of us.

'You heard the Doctor,' I yelled. 'Just shoot it!'

The Guardians pulled out their blasters and fired at the thing.

'Brilliant!' enthused the Doctor. 'Just as I thought. No effect. That's splendid. That means you have to listen to me if you want to live.'

'What?' Bentley stared at him in disbelief.

'Your guns don't work,' the Doctor was saying, 'and shortly after that happens, everyone always decides they need me—'

One of the Guardians got too close. She vanished screaming into the black mass. Seconds later something wet was thrown out of it.

'Trust me. Trust me now,' snapped the Doctor. 'You can't stop that creature. We all need to run.'

Bentley glanced in horror at the Guardian's body. At the black, glinting, whirring mass heading towards us.

'Fall back,' she snapped.

We all ran then, following the Doctor, who ran quickly, like he'd had a lifetime of running.

Bentley drew up to me. 'So, you're trusting 428 now?' she said.

'For the moment, I have to.'

'Don't be fooled,' she told me. 'Remember the report on him. He gets close to you so that he can attack you.'

'And what about you?' My voice was terse. 'Isn't that what you've done?'

'I was…' Bentley faltered. Or maybe she was running out of breath. 'I was obeying Protocols.'

The Doctor took us round a corner, and waited until we'd passed through an archway. As soon as the last Guardian was through, the Doctor brought up his spoon and a blast shield slammed down. Seconds later, the shield buckled under a terrific impact. The creature itself was utterly silent, but the metal it was attacking screamed.

'We do not…' the Doctor began and then his eyes drifted to the blast shield. All of us were watching it. 'We really don't have very long. It's got a lot stronger.'

Bentley marched up to him and knocked him to the floor. 'You let that thing loose on us. Because of you, another one of my Guardians is dead. When are you going stop?'

'People keep on hitting me today.' The Doctor lay sprawled on the floor. 'You know what, it's comfortable down here. I may stay.'

Bentley kicked him before I could stop her.

He groaned. 'Yes,' he said to her sourly. 'Yes, I let that thing out. Risky short cut. I am sorry about your colleague. If you'd listened to me, maybe it wouldn't have happened. But I needed to show you. You don't really know what's going on here at all. Ignore what you've been promised.'

'Shut up!' Bentley grabbed hold of him by the throat. When she spoke to him it was in a hoarse, exhausted scream. 'I don't care about your lies. Tell me about your creature!'

He let out a little rattle, flapping his hands at her arms. 'I can't,' he croaked. 'Not when you're… choking… me…'

But Bentley didn't let go. She was still shouting at him. 'It's all because of you, isn't it? Because of you they all died. I thought it was him –' she jabbed a finger at me – 'but no. The prisoners. Level 7. Chandress – yes, that was the name of "my colleague". I knew all their names – and… and…'

'Donaldson,' I said to Bentley, softly. I placed a hand on her shoulder. 'That's enough.' I spoke calmly. It was my best Governing tone.

For once, it sort of worked. She let go of the Doctor's throat. He fell back gasping. 'You… you've got quite a grip.'

Bentley turned to me, staring at me. Properly looking me in the eyes. Working out what I was going to say next.

'All right, then, *Governor*, what do you want to say? What are your orders?'

'Well…' I began. And then I saw it. The looks in her Guardians' faces. Their dismay that Bentley might listen to me. I'd lost their faith. I saw that now. And I couldn't afford for her to lose theirs. There had to be a chain of command of some sort.

'I don't… I don't have any orders.' My throat was dry, but I pressed on, pointing at them. 'Right now, I just want you to leave us alone. Prisoner 428 and I are working on a theory. That something's going on here that we don't understand yet. But that's it. I don't want you to obey me. Or even really believe me. I just want you all to stay alive and keep safe.'

I put down my hand, and pulled the Doctor up from the floor. He stared at me, still panting from Bentley's assault.

'Come on, Doctor,' I said. 'We're going.'

We walked away. No one tried to stop us.

We turned the corner.

The Doctor looked at me. 'Small thing,' he said. 'I should probably just nip back and tell them three more little facts.'

My hand landed on his shoulder. It was a modification of Safe Restraint Grip Five. The Doctor winced.

'On second thoughts,' he grunted, 'I don't think we need to go back after all.'

We walked on in silence. I took him to the viewing platform.

'Look at that,' I said. 'Out there. Space. Getting on with its life. All those planets and systems. All somehow moving on. It makes what's happening here… so trivial. Out there it's business as usual. In here… oh, I feel… is everything that's happened here somehow my fault?'

'Is it?' asked the Doctor.

'I don't know,' I told him. 'Not any more.'

'Well then…' He pointed out at the stars. 'I'll tell you something, Governor. Out there? That beautiful sparkling night sky? Every twinkle out there is putting a brave face on it. Each one's got their own problems. And I'll get to them all some day. But right now you're my priority.'

It felt comforting.

We stood and looked at the skies.

'So what do we do now?'

'I'll tell you a theory, if you'll then tell me something.'

'All right,' I agreed. I was searching the view, trying to see any traces of the remains of Level 7.

'My theory is that this Prison has been sabotaged. The power outages? The thing downstairs? The Custodians deactivating? The Defence Array firing when it shouldn't have? They're all part of that. A deliberate plan.'

'By who?'

'Have you any enemies, Governor?'

I laughed at that. 'Only friends,' I assured the Doctor. 'I've told you that. Everyone here is my friend.'

We both chuckled grimly.

'I'm wondering something,' I said. 'You're suggesting that somehow The Prison is turning against us.'

'I am, yes.'

'So that would mean that our TransNet linkup has been kept deliberately bad…'

'To avoid you being able to get help, yes.'

'Which would mean that this has been planned for

a long time. Maybe while The Prison was still being built?'

'Almost.' The Doctor tipped a hand out and tilted it from side to side. 'Some and some. I think we can agree on one thing, Governor, and that is that you've been set up. Set up for an almighty fall.'

I looked out at the stars. Then I held on to the rail. Very tightly.

'I'm not sure I can take another one,' I said. Then I sat down.

The Doctor stood behind me.

'It's OK,' he said. 'Take all the time you need.'

I nodded to him gratefully. The stars were still spinning. My world had collapsed. I remembered what had happened the last time I'd spoken to my wife. Had that been when it had all started?

Something clicked. Something in the long-ago faraway distance.

'You know I said take all the time you need?' came the Doctor's voice.

I nodded.

'Well,' the Doctor coughed, 'I lied. Get up. They've come for us.'

From the walls all around us, Custodians emerged.

'The good news…' began the Doctor.

There's good news?

'Theoretically, yes.' We were drawing together warily as the line of Custodians swept towards us.

'It's another line in my theory. Unless I'm very much mistaken, the Custodians have now been reactivated. The bad news is that they are now programmed to attack every living thing. If you'd – ah—' Each Custodian emitted a threatening buzzing sound. 'If you'd care to test my notion by walking up to them, then…'

'No, thank you. I'll believe you.'

'Capital!' The Doctor nodded, and ran a hand through his hair. 'See the bond of trust we've built up between us. Any ideas?'

'Can you use your spoon on them?'

The Doctor laughed shortly. 'It's just a spoon. It's only got two settings. Three if you're eating soup.'

'Well, there's nowhere to run.'

'No.'

The Custodians drew closer.

'Surrender?'

Sharp spokes sprang from each Custodian.

'I think not.'

Neither of us said anything for a moment.

'I've more good news for you,' I said. 'When Bentley finds our bodies, she'll know you were right.'

'Yes. That is indeed good news.'

The Custodians were two metres from us. The knives had been joined by pincers.

'At least…' I said, my mouth dry, 'it'll be quick.'

'Really?'

'No.'

'Thought not.' The Doctor shrugged, and in doing so, drew a jar of metal filings from his pocket. He threw them up into the air, where they hung like glitter. And then, from his other pocket, he brought out the blowtorch. It squirted a brief jet of flame. Not really enough to do anything other than ignite the fluttering glitter. Which burned, burned with a fierce light and heat.

The Doctor grabbed me, snatching me out of the way.

'Magnesium filings,' he said.

The burning cloud settled on the Custodians. And carried on burning. Their arms flew up, swatting them as they burned at their casings.

'I grabbed them from the workshop,' he explained.

'Is there anything you haven't stolen?'

'Hmm. Depends. What's not nailed down?'

The Custodians buzzed and banged against each other. The Doctor threw up more filings and ignited them. This time as they fell, a force shield flared up around the Custodians.

'They're protecting themselves. Which is good, because…'

The force shield flared, and the Custodians shut down.

The Doctor folded his arms. 'Thought so. They've not had a chance to properly recharge. Never launch a killing spree on an empty battery. Come on.'

We had to edge through them. Even powered down, there was something sinister about them. They still hummed with residual energy. I had to brush past a set of claws and spikes, feeling my uniform snag against them. I moved on, and then couldn't. A Custodian's claw had fastened around my uniform, seizing my arm.

'Doctor…' I hissed.

The claw was spasming, never quite releasing, never quite clamping down fully. I knew that if it did, it would cut clean through the bone.

The Doctor turned and looked. 'That one's got more charge than the others. A little. Not much.'

'Not helping.'

'Fine,' The Doctor was giving off the air of having bigger problems to deal with than me losing an arm. 'I'll do a thing. When I do the thing, I want you to run to the door and not stop. Not for anything.'

'Right.'

'Oh, and shut your eyes.'

'Why?'

'Cos if this goes wrong, you won't want to see.'

'Won't want to see what?'

The Doctor produced his spoon. He coughed, 'The electromagnet has two poles,' he said, tapping the battery taped to the base. 'Which gives me a fifty-fifty chance. If I get it right, that claw springs wide apart. If

I get it wrong…'

'Oh.'

'Sorry.'

'Are you sure about this?'

'Fifty-fifty isn't bad odds. I'd go so far as to offer you sixty-forty.'

'On what basis?'

'None whatsoever. You see, it's based on my purely reductive belief that things will work out for the best.' With a smile, the Doctor pounced on the claw. Before I could even scream.

Instinctively, I cried out and shut my eyes.

'You're done,' the Doctor whispered in my ear.

'Done how?'

'Done as in run.'

'My arms?'

'Still plural. Run.'

I opened my eyes. All I could see was the floor, without an arm lying flapping spare on it. So I ran for the door. As I did so, the Custodian behind me spun round into life and advanced on the Doctor.

'Down, boy,' he roared and aimed a strident kick at it.

The Custodian gave a loud clang and stopped. The Doctor cried out, hopping back from it, agonised.

'Did you hear that?' he wailed.

'The clang?'

'The crunch, man, the crunchy snapping sound.'

'No.'

The Doctor was windmilling his arms while swinging a foot back and forth.

'That was my toe.' He pulled an agonised face. 'That... that really hurt. I think I've broken my toe.'

'The Custodians are very solidly built. That was in the contract.'

'Dandy. Just dandy. The one thing here that is. Never mind. Let's get out of here.'

The Doctor hobbled off slowly, grimacing.

I followed him. Not quite sure where we were going.

It was silent on the launch pad. The Doctor eased himself into the chair I used to greet visitors.

'That's, actually, er, my chair...' I began, but the Doctor shot me a look. 'To which, of course, you're more than welcome.'

The Doctor slipped his boot off and examined his injured foot carefully. His sock was decorated with some surprisingly unexpected cartoon animals.

'This little piggy went to market... This little piggy stayed at home... This little piggy had roast beef... This little piggy had none... And this big piggy... arg.'

He waggled his toes and then smiled.

'What is it? Is your toe all right?

'No,' the Doctor's smile vanished. 'This piggy is quite definitely broken. But, see, when I move my toes it makes it look like the piggies are dancing. Ha.' He frowned. 'Where is she?'

'Clara?'

He nodded.

'I thought you said she was out here, protesting.' The Doctor narrowed his eyes.

'Frequently.'

'But the one time when I need her, she's away kissing, or teaching her children the rudimentary basics of transdimensional engineering. Typical. That girl… has no sense of priorities.' He sighed. 'That's the problem with companions. I had a dog once. Ah yes. That one worked out rather well.' He leaned back in the chair and shut his eyes. All of a sudden, he once more looked so old and so very tired.

There was a cough.

Clara was standing on the other side of the fence. The Doctor sprang to his feet, wincing only slightly.

'Clara Ostrich!' The Doctor beamed.

'The surname is Oswald,' said Clara.

'Well, I've been thinking. About the surname. You never really liked it, I've never really liked it. And Ostrich is much better. Because of the neck.'

Clara considered him coolly. 'I've missed you,' she said.

'And I've missed you too.'

They stood there for a moment, grinning at each other like idiots.

'Ooh, nice socks,' said Clara.

'Socks don't matter,' said the Doctor, slipping the boot gingerly back on. 'So, it's you and me back together again. The Doctor and Clara. Separated only by an electrical fence.'

'Plus seventy-three other security systems,' I put in.

'And I'll get to those in a minute,' the Doctor dismissed me. Now that Clara was here, I got the feeling I was no longer important. Curious. He was studying her intently. 'Now then, Ostrich, you're late. You're never late. There's a reason, isn't there?' He smiled at her.

Clara nodded. 'The TARDIS and I have been on a side trip.'

'Nice to see the two of you getting along.' The Doctor beamed. 'The TARDIS is my spaceship,' he explained to me. He dropped his voice to a stage whisper. 'She and Clara never used to be friendly. But they've managed to forget and forgive.'

'I've not forgotten!' protested Clara.

'And I'm sure the TARDIS hasn't forgiven,' said the Doctor. 'Now where have you been, you old sly-boots?'

'Weelll…' Clara twisted on her feet, clearly pleased with herself but also a little worried about the impact her news would have. 'Do be pleased—'

'I rarely am these days.'

'OK.' She took a deep breath. 'We rescued the people on Level 7.'

'You did what?' I cried, and nearly threw myself on the electric fence in an attempt to embrace her.

'You did what?' The Doctor's tone was less joyous. 'Tell me you didn't travel back in time and save them?'

Clara shook her head. 'As it flew past, we detected the Defence Array powering up, so we hopped over, loaded them in, and then dropped them off on a colony. Hence the delay.' For some reason I wasn't quite sure of, she was holding her hand behind her back. 'Nice little world called Birling.'

I reacted to that. I'd hoped never to hear the name again.

'I see,' the Doctor looked at her, and then at me. 'Well, one less massacre. And I'm sure the Oracle will be pleased.'

'Is that…' Clara wrinkled her nose distastefully. 'Is that the weird fat bloke doing the invisible knitting? Before the people on the colony locked him up, he told me I'd meet a tall, dark stranger and go on a long journey.'

The Doctor beamed. 'Well, that's pretty right, isn't it? For once?'

'When do I get tall and dark again?'

The Doctor scowled. 'I have rather missed you,' he said.

'We've done that bit.'

'Right then, what's next on the list? Oh yes, the fun, impressive moment.'

'I always like that bit.'

They kept on like this for a bit, and I was rather glad I wasn't sat behind them on a long shuttle journey. I almost wanted to be a part of their world, while worried at how they could behave like it in the middle of chaos.

At the same time, I was swamped with relief. Level 7 was fine. Everyone was fine. They'd lived. For the first time that day, I knew that things were going to be all right. Because the Doctor and Clara were here.

Which was when half of the landing pad exploded.

Clara was thrown screaming to the ground. She scrambled up, debris and flame swirling around her.

'What?' she cried.

'The Defence Array…' I stammered. 'But why?'

The weapon fired again. The ground between us and Clara burned.

'It's now turned in on The Prison,' said the Doctor. 'It's detected the arrival of Clara. And it's quite determined to wipe her out. And most especially our spaceship.'

There was another blast. Closer to Clara.

'It's still calibrating,' mused the Doctor. 'Seventy-three systems keeping her out?'

'And the fence. Yes.'

'Turn them off. Let her in. Now.'

'I can't,' I protested.

The Defence Array fired again. Clara was now

sheltering behind the small rock she'd sat on earlier. Chips of it were flying into the air.

'You have to.' The Doctor was fierce with urgency. 'Look at her!'

Clara shrank as more shots fell near her. The thin atmosphere was full of sparks.

'I just can't,' I protested. 'The system is designed to be impregnable. I can't let an innocent person in. I just can't.'

Another bolt split the stone in two. And then another shattered it.

With nowhere left to hide, Clara stood up, alone and exposed, covered in small cuts from the splinters of rock.

'Shall I run for the TARDIS?' she suggested.

'I'm afraid you won't make it,' said the Doctor. 'You don't stand a chance out there.'

'Goodbye?' she offered.

'Never,' the Doctor was firm. He turned to me. 'The innocent can't come in, you say?'

'Yes,' I confirmed.

'How innocent?'

'Good point.' I laughed suddenly. 'Clara, could you hit that sign there, please?'

'This one?' The notice said 'DO NOT TOUCH THE FENCE.'

'Yes. Very hard.'

Clara threw a lump of rock at it. The sign dented.

'Clara Ostrich,' I intoned over the blasts of the Defence Array, 'in my capacity as Governor –' the Doctor was making 'hurry up' motions – 'I arrest you for damaging prison property. Come inside.'

The fence sprang open and Clara hurried in. As it shut, the Defence Array scoured the landing pad where she'd been standing. The firestorm behind us was blinding.

We stood there, catching our breath. Despite her previous aloofness, Clara was shaking. The Doctor held her to him.

'That is kind of a hug,' he said. 'You know I don't do hugging.'

'The old one did,' she told him.

'Ah well.' He let her go. 'Curious custom. Though I suppose it's a good way of smelling hair. You've changed shampoo.'

'Shampoo?' She stepped back.

'Could be important later,' he considered, then discarded, the thought. 'No, probably not.'

'I don't think,' I said to the Doctor, 'that you take things seriously enough.'

'On the contrary,' the Doctor retorted, 'I think the universe takes itself far too seriously.' He stuck his hands in his pockets and looked at us both. 'So, we have to find out what's going on, make this prison safe and then save an entire system.'

'We do?' I asked.

Clara nodded. 'It's epic. And it's what we do. I'm very good at it. He's… fine.'

'I've very good. Look,' said the Doctor proudly, producing an object from his pocket. 'I've got a sonic spoon.'

Clara gave him a look. It wasn't exactly impressed.

There was another blast from the Defence Array. The fence melted along with the wall behind us.

'One thing,' said the Doctor. 'Right now everything in this prison wants to kill us. The external defences. The internal defences. And something deep inside that's very large and mysterious. Someone wants to make very sure that we die.'

'Well, I must say, I've missed you,' said Clara.

The Defence Array fired again, and we started to run before we were atomised.

9

As the corridor behind us was burned away, we were running for our lives.

Or rather, Clara and I were running, and the Doctor was hobbling.

'What's wrong?' asked Clara.

The Doctor appeared to be cursing under his breath. 'Nothing,' he muttered, wincing as he placed his weight on his foot.

'Doesn't look like nothing. Have you been shot in the leg or something?'

The Doctor shook his head, sheepish. 'Nothing. Carry on, let's keep going.' He lurched on at a strange sort of leaping limp.

'So, what's happened to your foot?'

'I, uh…' The Doctor glared at me for support.

'He was saving my life,' I put in.

'How?'

The Doctor muttered again.

Clara's eyes narrowed. 'Did you just say you

stubbed your toe?'

The Doctor nodded and whispered something else. 'I think I've broken it.'

'Your toe?'

'Is broken, yes.'

'That's a bit rubbish, isn't it?'

'No.' A pause. 'It's the big toe.'

'Can't you, you know… do the thing?'

The Doctor glared at her, an angry owl zeroing in on a shrew. 'You're suggesting I regenerate simply because I've stubbed my toe?'

'Can't you?'

'Well, I could, but it seems a bit of a waste of a life.'

'Can't you just do the toe?'

'Regeneration is a prized miracle of Time Lord physiognomy and you're saying I use it to renew my toe?'

'It was just a suggestion.'

'Well, no. I can't. Since you ask.'

'That's a bit of a limitation.'

'Tell you what, I'll write them a letter.'

'Do so.'

They carried on in this baffling way for a bit, bickering fondly as they ran.

'Is this sort of thing going to happen more often now that you're—'

'Don't say it,' snapped the Doctor. 'No, actually, do go on. Now that I'm what?'

'Distinguished. As in old.'

'No. I hope not. And anyway, I'm only in my early thousands. That's nothing.'

'It's just we could look at getting you one of those mobility scooter things. My nan has one.'

'No.'

'She swears by it. You can fit the shopping in it.'

'No.' The Doctor limped on. 'And anyway. I already have a trolley somewhere.'

We rounded a corner. I was completely out of breath, Clara was grinning, and the Doctor seemed to be insisting on his unusual wobbling gait.

'I dunno,' announced Clara. 'Last time I saw you, you were the valiant saviour of worlds. Now you have a magic spoon and a dodgy toe. Back home, you'd be hanging around outside the supermarket bins.'

The Doctor looked at me for reassurance. 'This! This is what I have to put up with. Honestly, prison has been, in some ways, a lovely break.'

The entire floor shuddered and tipped. We all slid and fell.

'What's happening?' I yelled, holding on to a support strut as the world spun around me.

'Well, I dunno,' muttered the Doctor. 'Perhaps the Defence Array's hit one of the support struts, or it could be the artificial gravity failing.'

The floor gave another creak and then twisted sideways. The Doctor scrambled back to his feet and started limping rapidly off.

'What are you doing?'

'We need to be in a small space while the systems stabilise. Like a really tiny room. Luckily, this is a prison. There's not a shortage of tiny rooms. Come on.'

We followed him.

Three was a crowd in a cell.

'Cosy?' suggested the Doctor.

'Snug?' mused Clara.

The Doctor flung himself down on the bed, stretching out to fill it. Which left Clara and me squashed together by the door. Arms behind his head, staring up at the ceiling, the Doctor seemed to be ignoring us. '*Cells I Have Known*. That's what I'd call it. Or *My Life Behind Bars*. But I'll definitely find time to write some kind of guide to the various prisons I've been held in one of these days. I'd give them stars – I love stars. Don't you love stars?'

'I love stars,' agreed Clara.

'Categories. That's the other thing. Location? Ambience? Ease of Escape?' He paused. 'Sense of Hopelessness? Screams of Other Prisoners? Inventiveness of Torture?'

He sat up, trying the weight on his toe, and winced. 'Thing is, what's the point? A prison cell is just a bare minimum. The littlest amount of space you need to let life continue. A confinement, but also an awareness of everything you're missing. Wouldn't you agree, Governor?' He stared right at me.

'Yes,' I said, my mouth suddenly dry. There were so many other things we could be doing now, but for some reason, this felt very important. 'Are you complaining? I've tried my best here. To be humane. Within the Protocols.'

I really had. I mean, if you ignored the little exceptions. The people I enjoyed punishing. Because of what they'd done.

'You know what? I don't care any more.' The Doctor yawned. 'You can justify yourself as much as you want. Boring. It's not why I'm here.'

'Can I remind you, Doctor, you're here because you committed dreadful crimes.'

'Did I?'

'Oh please,' I grunted. 'Everyone's innocent.'

'Ah yes.' The Doctor clapped his hands together and the noise was sharp and loud. 'But what if I really was? What if I'd been stitched up, grassed up and banged up?'

'No, don't do that,' whispered Clara, embarrassed.

'But I can.' The Doctor beamed. 'I'm an old lag. A vicious criminal. Apparently. Unless, of course, I'm totally innocent. And you've just been told I'm a criminal. The one lie you'd believe.'

I can't remember crossing the room. I really can't.

But there I was. Suddenly, shouting in his face. All of the careful training, the instructions to hide as much of yourself as possible, all of that. Gone.

'I don't care, Doctor. I really don't. You want to lie to yourself to get through the day? Fine. But don't bother with me. I know what you've really done. Why they sent you here. And you're going to pay for that some day, I'll make sure of it. I know, no one's all good. Or all evil. You've done great good here – but I know what you did before. And that's why you're never getting out of this place. I'll make sure of it. This prison can tear itself apart and you'll never leave it. Until there's nothing left. You'll stay here. And I'll be here with you.'

'Why?' asked the Doctor. 'What have I done?'

'Don't bother,' I snapped.

Clara stood between us. The uncertainty on her face told me all I needed to know. She didn't quite believe in his innocence either. His best friend. His champion. And she was worried.

The Doctor turned away, dismissing us both. 'Doesn't matter,' he snapped. 'Clara, did you bring the papers with you?' He flapped a hand, 'Oh, I know, it's smuggling. Get her, she's quite the criminal. But it's important.'

Clara reached into her jacket and produced a plastic wallet with printouts from TransNet newscasts. 'You don't get much news here, do you?' she asked gently.

'Not really,' I said, 'We don't have the bandwidth. And, at this distance, it seems trivial. The squabbles and sadnesses of people I will never see again.'

'Well, you should read this.'

I flicked through the folder. The headlines made my heart flicker, just a little. The HomeWorld Government was in trouble. The new president was increasingly unpopular. There were protests and riots. Good, I thought. I tried not to gloat. But GOOD.

'Ah well, what does it matter?' I sighed. 'They'll find someone else to rule them. Someone even worse.'

The Doctor was staring at me again, measuring my reaction. 'Really? Who?' he asked.

'Someone weak. Someone who gets out of his depth and makes the wrong decision. Who does something unforgiveable. Someone human.'

A silence settled over us. Clara was watching me as well.

'It doesn't matter, not really,' I said.

More awkward silence.

'Sure?' said the Doctor eventually.

'I think we're all agreed that, whatever my failings as a prison governor,' I sighed, 'that I was an even worse HomeWorld president.'

10

Turns out, it's really easy to rig an election. First you just murder my wife.

'I'm sorry,' said Clara.

But that wasn't good enough for the Doctor. 'Nice soundbite, but no. It wasn't that simple, was it?'

Well, it wasn't quite that simple. But it was fairly easy.

My re-election should have been reasonably straightforward, but then someone on the opposition… well, no, that's unfair. Perhaps I should say 'someone with interests not unallied to those of my political opponents'… Someone realised that the weak spot was in the outer colonies. Specifically that it was just a matter of flipping the voting habits of one or two.

They started by picking the world of Birling and an almost extinct disease. It was called Lopo, which is a stupid little name for a disease. Centuries ago it was lethal, now it was almost unheard of. Children on Birling were immunised against Lopo as a matter of course, but all of a sudden there weren't enough supplies of vaccine. Just a tiny hiccup at a HomeWorld production facility. Then the smallest of delays over the shipping of those supplies across the System as they went through Customs.

Luckily, the private sector stepped in to help out Birling. Only it turned out that some of the vaccines they supplied were out of date, or watered down.

From out of nowhere a crank without even a proper medical degree – a Professor of Acupuncture and Astrology (you can work out who that was for yourselves) – started giving media interviews on Birling, saying that the vaccine caused growth deficiency. It was completely unsupported by fact. But the fraud made compelling television. All of a sudden, parents on Birling were holding up their toddlers and saying to each other 'She does, you know, look a little small, don't you think… Perhaps we'd better not vaccinate her little brother…' It was utter nonsense, but we had a free and fair press, so when MedAuth put up a doctor to explain the facts, up would pop the Professor of Acupuncture and Nonsense as well. To establish balance. And people thought 'Well, there must be something in it. Otherwise they wouldn't be talking about it on the TransNet.'

It took a while for the MedAuth on HomeWorld to

realise the size of the problem. There weren't enough Lopo vaccines for the children of Birling. And parents weren't bringing their children in to be immunised to receive the few ampoules that had cleared customs. It wasn't long before the first cases of Lopo started to be reported. My wife held the position of Honorary Chair of MedAuth. Because she looked very good hugging babies. We'd never had children of our own, but Helen held a stranger's infant like it was a diamond of joy.

So my wife went to Birling, to try and reassure the population about the vaccine and the dangers of Lopo. The virus was still there on the planet, but, she'd been vaccinated as an infant. However, denied a proper chance to feed, Lopo had been mutating. First the children caught it. Then it jumped to adults who had been immunised against it.

My opponents had merely intended to create a situation where enough people on Birling were dealing with their sick children to not bother voting. Instead they'd caused a lethal epidemic. My wife was caught up in the quarantine. Helen made the best of it, travelling across Birling, trying her best to sort out the situation. Of course she got sick.

Suddenly, the impending election really was the last thing on my mind. I'd talk to her on TransNet every day. That was all my advisers would allow me to do. I was all for jumping on board a shuttle to Birling and going to her, spending all the time that Helen had left. But 'No, sir,' they said. 'We forbid it. You have to think about the election. You owe your wife a great deal, of course, but you owe the people of the HomeWorld even more.'

What a fatuous, pompous idiot I must have been to have even listened to them. But I did. I looked noble. I suffered in public. And, when the time came, I wore black very sombrely.

The problem about the epidemic on Birling was that the causes for it were reasonably simple. But it was even easier to blame me. Worse, at exactly the same time as I was being attacked for not supplying enough Lopo vaccine, parents on other worlds were looking at their children and saying, 'He does, you know, look a little small, don't you think…? Perhaps we'd better not vaccinate his sister…'

Sickeningly, the death of my wife provided me with what my advisers called a 'Sympathy Bump' in the opinion polls. But my increased popularity wasn't going to be enough for me to win the election. I could see that, and I was prepared to admit defeat. I didn't, to be truthful, want to carry on any more.

But then my Chief Adviser came to see me. Her name was Marianne Globus. My wife had always suspected us of… I'm not sure. Of having an affair? Certainly we flirted, but Marianne was like one of those flowers you went to see in an arboretum. When lavishly cared for, she flourished with rare beauty, but you couldn't imagine taking one home.

Marianne talked me out of not contesting the election. She also pointed out that the opposition had, in effect, cheated me out of votes. A lot of votes. And what she was proposing was not rigging the election, not at all. It was simply a slight statistical correction. That was the phrase she used. When I protested, she reassured me: 'Don't worry, it's just the little people. They don't count.'

The plan was simple. Identify a few outlying polling stations that were too remote to have observers posted there. If they were manual, simply ensure an extra box of statistically corrected ballots were posted. It they had voting machines, ensure that the software worked to assist the undecided to vote in our favour.

A few people noticed, of course, and there was some outcry at my re-election, muted by my status as a widower. I spoke out against the unfounded allegations, pointed to the sour grapes of the opposition, capitalising on my grief. I insisted that elections had been done in accordance with regulations. At the same time I announced plans for the building of The Prison. Nothing suggested that Law and Order were at the top of your agenda more than saying you were going to build a really big prison. It helped that I could put a few of my opponents in there. Along with the Professor of Acupuncture and

Astrology on Birling. It showed I was in command. Everything settled down.

The problem was that a very bright TransNet correspondent had spotted the statistical correction. Or rather, he'd spotted how precise it was. The mistake that Marianne had made was to provide exactly the right number of votes from each of our tampered polling stations. It was an error of fairness on her part – rather than provide a landslide victory she simply gave me just enough to win.

The journalist started asking questions. He was blocked at every stage by my legal counsel. The problem was, it just wouldn't go away. And then the defeated opposition jumped on this.

Marianne ordered me to 'get behind' the problem. I issued a denial and promised an inquiry. The inquiry would be run by my legal counsel's tutor, a brilliant and respected law professor called Lafcardio. Lafcardio was a very clever man, but also rather unworldly, preferring the company of books to people. He went into the inquiry with the simple belief that a nice, grieving widower just wouldn't be the sort of person to rig an election, and it was almost as though he didn't notice any evidence pointing the other way.

Lafcardio exonerated me. He did so rather too well. I was too busy formally acknowledging I had been cleared to notice that the people didn't believe it for a moment.

The opposition suddenly became a protest movement with the voice of the people leading it.

I tried defusing the situation. I fired Marianne Globus. I issued a brief apology of sorts. You know the kind of thing: 'I must regret that some people have perceived that there was any irregularity. While I remain assured of the absolute integrity of the decision of the hard-working electorate, I must also say that I am disappointed in the clarity of the information provided to me by one single adviser. I trust that this is an end of the matter.'

It wasn't. The people rose up. And the opposition, the people who had killed my wife and spread a plague through the outer colonies, were swept into power.

The Prison had begun construction under my reign, but it was hastily finished by the opposition, handing out contracts to their allies. After a series of show trials, almost my entire government were placed in The Prison. A few were allowed to remain on HomeWorld to form a puppet opposition, their obedience assured by the presence of their loved ones in Level 7. And, as the ultimate humiliation, I was placed here as Governor of The Prison. The jailer of my former friends.

I tried to do my best. But then so many more inmates started to arrive. And I never knew who was guilty, and who was innocent. I don't know any more.

The one thing they never told me, the thing I never found out, was exactly who caused the plague. Who came to my opponents with the idea. Who carried it out. Who was the mastermind who wiped out all those people. Who killed my wife.

And then, one day, they sent him to me. The greatest criminal ever. The one person I could never forgive.

The Doctor.

'Ah,' said the Doctor. 'Well, that all makes sense now.'

'Are you going to apologise?' All the anger I'd tried to keep down all these years swelled up suddenly behind my eyes in a red fury.

The Doctor didn't seem that bothered. He shrugged. 'No. I didn't do it.'

'Prove it.'

'Really?' the Doctor groaned. 'I can't. Only… it's always easy to see a great mastermind at work behind things. And they do exist – believe me, I've met quite a few. But the thing is, people are such frail, weak beings. It doesn't need a man twirling a black cape. Some of the worst decisions in history have been made in rooms by people who meant well. There's a reason they say nothing good ever came out of a committee. Beware of Focus Groups, Working Parties, Conference Calls, and people who find ninety-nine reasons to say no before they find a single reason to say yes. It's these people who are responsible for most of the evil in the universe. And it's why they're all unaccountable. None of them can ever remember making the big, awful decision. No one person decided to build a Death Ray. Perhaps someone can remember making some useful tweaks to the firing nozzle, a few good suggestions at an away day about the Death Ray logo, or perhaps deciding that the nice big button should be red… but… oh, I'm always asked what the end of the universe will be like. It'll be a room full of people fighting politely over the last chocolate biscuit as they squeeze in one final meeting about how terribly dark it's getting.'

He'd stopped talking. For some reason I was crying. I couldn't believe what he was saying. I just couldn't. It was just flippant noise.

'You're saying it wasn't you?' My voice sounded really calm. Somewhere inside my head though, my soul was shouting HOW DARE YOU? HOW DARE YOU? *HOW DARE YOU?*

'No,' Clara spoke. Her voice was very firm. 'You won't believe him. But you'll believe me. Won't you?'

'Oh yes, I always believe the cranky fans,' I snapped.

'It's her wide eyes, isn't it?' suggested the Doctor unflappably. 'I've had words.'

'Oi!' Clara stood up, defiant, climbing onto the table-shelf. 'Listen to me. We arrived in this system just when it was all going wrong for the new regime. The plague had spread, the outer colonies were being kept going by supply ships. And suddenly, there was a suggestion by the authorities that, well, it was costing a lot to supply these ships and that, perhaps HomeWorld should look after its own first. HomeWorldFirst. That was the name of the movement.'

'Horrible,' I said.

'HomeWorldFirst had rallies. They didn't want to leave the colonies to die, no, not at all. They just wanted to introduce a Contribution Assessment. Basically, to find out what each colony brought in in return for continued supplies of vaccines…'

'But… but… they caused the plague in the first place!' I protested.

'Yes. But HomeWorldFirst were very persuasive.'

'And that's what made the people rise up?' I felt a sudden surge of pride.

Clara pulled a face, 'Actually, it was over the plans to build a shopping centre on a park, but that did it. A protest movement that even the Government couldn't control. Suddenly the people of HomeWorld got their political mojo on. It's not been pretty – we've both of us been caught up in the fighting for some time. The Doctor's done his best, but it's been anarchy. Literally.'

'The one good thing,' the Doctor said, 'is that all the

best mercenaries from the last conflict were locked up in here. HomeWorld's been trying to get them out, but as they made sure there was no system for getting people out of here, it all got hopelessly tangled in paperwork. That's the problem with running things by committee.'

'So, no bloodshed?'

'Well, some…' said Clara. 'But turns out that the new lot really aren't very popular any more. It's one thing to order your soldiers to go out and fire on protesters. But when the protesters are your own grandparents… There were a few idiots who opened fire anyway. But not many. The old regime is crumbling. Very fast indeed. They thought they'd scored a coup when they arrested the Doctor. An alien. Clearly an alien ringleader.'

'Actually, just a tourist.' The Doctor shrugged. 'I keep telling people. Really. I've done nothing but sightseeing.'

'Really?' Clara gazed at him proudly. 'What do you call saving that hospital from the missile?'

'A day trip.' The Doctor tried to look modest. It didn't suit him.

'The thing is,' Clara continued, 'the Government have known since they put you all in here that you're the only credible alternative to them. It didn't matter when they were still popular. But, all of a sudden, they're not, and now you're a threat. They thought they were being somehow humane putting you here. But they weren't stupid. They no longer needed Level 7. They no longer needed any of you.'

'As I've been telling you –' the Doctor stood up painfully, limping a little as he waved his arms around like a general in a play – 'the Prison systems have been reset. They're no longer here to protect you. They're here to wipe all of you out. The Guardians think they're in on it, but they're just an embarrassing amount of evidence. They're for the chop as well.'

'But what about that creature?'

'A guilty conscience?' The Doctor smiled. 'There's something hidden here. It has been all along.'

'What do you mean?'

'I think,' mused the Doctor, 'this prison has one last surprise to spring on us. And we've got to find it before it finds us.'

11

The corridors were dark. The Prison was eerie. Making our way through it was uncertain. I really didn't know what to think of anything, really. I almost didn't trust the ground beneath my feet. Which, if you think about it, was fair enough. It really was all just artificial – it was only the ground because the artificial gravity told me to think of it that way. I couldn't be sure that it would still be the ground from one foot to the next. As we went up the stairs, the Doctor winced on each step. He counted them aloud as he dragged himself along. 'Interesting,' he grunted, but didn't elaborate.

We passed the bodies of Guardians. There'd clearly been a huge fight between them and the Custodians.

'No prisoners,' I said. We hadn't seen any inmates' bodies among the fallen or in their cells. I presumed we would, somehow. It wasn't too fanciful to hope they'd join up with the Guardians against the Custodians.

'Actually, where are the Custodians?' I asked.

We were stood in a hallway. Up above us the

stairwell spiralled. All of the corridors above us were empty. You'd normally see Custodians gliding from cell to cell, or docked in the walls. But there was none of that.

The Doctor seemed pleased. 'I'm all in favour of an absence of killer robots.'

'Um,' said Clara. 'Only… well, where have they gone?'

The Doctor's face fell. 'Good point. Where?'

I took them to the Control Station. The place had been gutted. At first it looked like sabotage, but then it became clear it had been systematically stripped. Screens dangled blankly. Empty keyboards hung from desks, most of the computers behind them gone or wrecked.

I went to my office. The place was empty. My records had gone. My terminal had gone. Even the rosebush the Doctor had brought me was smashed, a tangle of severed buds lying among spilt earth and broken pottery. The Doctor picked up a stray flower, picking at the petals sadly.

'Someone's cleaned this place out thoroughly.'

'Human or robot?'

'A little from Column A, a little from Column B,' mused the Doctor.

We found Bentley holed up in the TransNet Room.

It was more of a cupboard, really. Once we'd realised how feeble the link was, we'd given it its own space. People who'd grown up used to the TransNet everywhere now came to terms with having it in a single room.

A single room with a solid door. That was barricaded.

Shots rang out from the window, and we threw ourselves to the ground.

'Go away,' yelled the voice. 'TransNet is mine now.'

I'd always found Bentley hard to deal with. Actually, that sentence can be shorter. I'd always found Bentley hard. No matter what I did, no matter how rigorously I followed procedure, there was always that feeling that I was a fake, that I didn't deserve the appointment.

She had a reasonable point. I didn't. But then again, when I was President of HomeWorld, I didn't feel any less of a phoney. At any moment, I felt sure that one of my ministers would expose me as a fool who didn't know what he was doing. Then again, it did turn out that they were all plotting against me. Which was, in some ways, reassuring, and in other ways, unhelpful.

Every day, Bentley did what she could to just gently remind me that I was just as much of a prisoner as my charges. It was why she never looked me in the eye. I knew that was the real reason why the TransNet did not work on my terminal. Why the Custodians occasionally hesitated – so very slightly – before obeying my commands. Why the Guardians rarely acknowledged me.

Bentley did not want me to feel secure. She was supposed to be Governor, but I'd stolen that from her, even though she ran the place. She'd never forgiven me. She wanted me to remember, every moment of the day, that this prison was my punishment, my humiliation. And that she was enjoying it.

Truthfully, in the early days, I really didn't need her to remind me of my despair. And then, as time moved on, I felt more secure. I was almost at peace with my exile.

True, my former friends could not forgive me. They saw me as a traitor. They could barely look at me either. And, of course, there was Marianne. Marianne who at first took prison stoically. And then cracked. She'd asked to see me. I remember Bentley showing her in, her eyebrow cocked as though to say, 'Oh, this'll be good'. My former special adviser stood before me, shaking, telling me she couldn't bear to be contained here any longer, that she had to be released.

I tried being soothing. I tried everything. But she wouldn't listen to reason. She just screamed at me until Bentley led her gently away, talking to her in calming tones. I thought it was going to be all right, but then came her awful, hideous escape attempt.

After that, well… the one good thing that came of it was that no one tried escaping again. Not until the arrival of the Doctor.

The Doctor was speaking to Bentley now. He was talking in a measured, reasoning voice.

'Bentley, listen to me. It's 428. We just want a chat.' He inched towards her, his limp exaggerated slightly, making him look a little pathetic.

'428 – You will address me as "Sir".'

'Are you sure you wouldn't prefer "Ma'am", ma'am?'

'"Sir". Unless you want to be shot.'

A small sigh. 'Well, all right, sir. Of course.' His hands were out, placating. 'You have a gun, sir. I have enormous respect for guns and the people who carry them. Always have.' He gave Clara a wink at this point and muttered to her. 'Clara. I'm going to need the full 3B from you in a moment.' What's he up to? I thought.

'Listen, sir, you and I both know how this is going to be. You have the gun. You have the barricaded door. You have control of the TransNet. You have all the power. And us? Well, what are we? A prisoner, a political failure, and a girl in a tea-dress.'

'Hello!' waved Clara.

Bentley's face appeared through the window in the door. She stared at Clara.

'Her? Where's she come from?' Bentley sounded more afraid than anything else.

'Oh…' Clara said. 'Outside. I'm technically on remand. Isn't that right?'

I nodded. 'She damaged prison property.'

'She's brought lies in with her,' snapped Bentley.

'Um, no,' said Clara. For a moment she looked a little cross. Then her sweet smile returned. She stepped forward, edging the Doctor out of the way. I realised that she wasn't at all afraid of the gun Bentley was pointing at her. 'Can I just check – you are in charge here, aren't you?'

'Yes.'

'I didn't think the Governor could be. I mean… not really. Well, look at him.'

I frowned, feeling a touch betrayed.

'No, he's never been in charge,' Bentley snarled. 'They told me he was, but it was easy to bypass him. To take command. He's weak.' Bentley spat the words out.

'Oh yes, yes, he is,' agreed Clara, soothingly. She was oddly close to the door. 'I'm a teacher, you know.' She was being lightly conversational. 'My class is full of boys like him. And they do all right… I suppose. Not wonderfully well, but not awfully. They get by on the minimum of homework. Just scraping through.'

'They do the reading, but they don't understand,' was Bentley's surprising contribution. 'I had a friend – Gillian.' I realised she was talking about Donaldson. How awful. I'd known her first name but never used it. 'Before she was a Guardian here she was a teacher. She said teaching boys was just like that.'

'Oh yes,' Clara nodded enthusiastically. 'The Doctor's the same as the boys in 3B, you know.'

The Doctor nodded seriously.

'So come on,' Clara went on. 'Just you and me… Tell me what's really going on here. I mean, they'd never spot it in a million years. They just don't understand.'

'Ah…' Bentley wasn't quite that stupid. 'Why should I tell you?' she sneered. 'You're working for the Doctor. You're his accomplice.'

Clara put her hands on her hips and laughed. It was a really charming laugh. When people say 'her face lit up' it's hard to tell what they mean until you really see it. I suddenly wished Helen and I had had a daughter. She'd have been just like Clara.

'I'm working for the Doctor?' She rolled her eyes and smiled with all of her ruby-red lips. 'Oh please. He works for me. He's my front man. Come on, if he really was in charge, do you think he'd have been stupid enough to get himself locked up?'

The Doctor made a noise.

'He makes a lot of noise and fuss. And I just quietly get on with running things.'

'I know just how you feel,' admitted Bentley. She'd swung the door open, standing behind her barricade of desks and chairs, facing Clara. She was still aiming the gun. Directly at Clara. If she'd fired it, Clara would have been pulp. But Clara just didn't care.

'Now then.' Clara was all business. 'I know that

you're not going to trust me. You're too smart to. But I'm betting that you're just about now realising that you've been... shall we say... a little let down by the HomeWorld? Am I right? You were clever enough to finally work out what was going on with the system failures, and they admitted it, and they led you to expect that, when The Prison shut down, all the Guardians would be rescued. Instead the Custodians have turned on all of you. And you're finding that no one back home is answering your alerts on the TransNet. Correct?'

Bentley looked at her for a long moment. 'Correct. We're cut off.'

'Right about now, the penny is dropping isn't it?' Clara puckered her face in coaxing sympathy.

'They don't want there to be any survivors. Any witnesses,' whispered Bentley hollowly. 'There's no escape from here. The only possibility was... was Level 7.'

Clara nodded. 'Don't worry about that. I rescued them all.'

'You're lying,' hissed Bentley.

'Well why would I?' snapped Clara. Her patience was wearing thin. 'Won't someone stop thinking of the children? I've had to share my ship with that creepy... oh what was his name... The Oracle? He kept trying to tell me my fortune and assuring everyone that he knew that was going to happen.

While crying with relief. Anyway, he says hello, by the way. And –' Clara's brow darkened – 'that you knew it would come under attack.'

'I couldn't stop it from happening,' said Bentley. 'I had no idea.' The statements were contradictory. I wondered how wrong I'd been to trust her at all at any point. She'd been working against me all along.

'I'm sure you did your best,' Clara said, shooting me a warning look. I was about to say something about how Bentley had herded people onto that ship and sent it off, thinking they were all going to die. But seeing Clara's look, I shut up.

'So…' Clara continued, 'Of course you did your best. And HomeWorld said that they'd come for you. But they're not coming, are they?'

'No…' admitted Bentley. 'And there's only a few hours before the systems shut down completely. Life support is already failing. The Defence Array is bombarding us. We may freeze. We may suffocate. We may get blown up. If the Custodians don't find us first.'

'It's not a problem, actually,' insisted Clara. 'I've still got my spacecraft.'

'No.' And here Bentley gloated. She always loved having an advantage over someone. 'I've seen what the Defence Array's done to the surface of this asteroid. It's scoured it. If it was on the landing pad, your ship will be dust.'

Clara shook her head. 'It's actually very resilient. Indestructible. Stubborn. It's the one reason why I keep the Doctor on as my driver. He's a hopeless pilot, but his ship… trust me… his ship is going nowhere. I can take you to it. Come on now,' she continued. 'Why not pop down the gun and come out, and you and I will go find my ship. Don't worry about my boys.' She indicated us. 'They'll stay well back.'

There was a pause, and then Bentley came out of the TransNet room, and surveyed Clara. She was still holding the gun, but it was by her side.

'I'll think I'll keep the gun,' announced Bentley firmly, but with a touch of the sulky child.

'Oh, I was sure of that,' said Clara, a touch sadly. 'You're the type. Come along. Let's go find the ship.' She turned back to the Doctor. 'You two, see if you can round any other survivors up. We'll see you back at the ranch.'

And then, calmly, they walked out of the Control Station.

The Doctor turned to me and let out a huge breath. 'I don't know what it is, but I just can't stand people with guns any more. I used to be able to handle it, but… I guess it's old age.' He hobbled painfully towards the TransNet booth. 'However, it's got us some access.'

'What about Clara?'

The Doctor limped forward, and hunched over the

TransNet terminal. 'She's using her full-on "Taking Class 3B for History" mode. She's bombproof like that.'

He pecked away at the keys, trying to get into the TransNet. 'Lovely,' he said. 'It's like a dial-up modem without the constant whining. But I think I'm about to find out what's going on back home. Just a few more seconds.'

Which was when we heard the screams from the corridor.

12

The long corridor outside was empty. There was no sign of Bentley or Clara. The Doctor stood at the intersection, shouting Clara's name. He made to run off, took a few stumbling steps, howled in pain and frustration, and then pulled up to a halt, limping back to me. His face thundered.

'You!' His finger jabbed at me. 'This is all your fault.'

'Probably,' I agreed with him glumly. 'How exactly?'

'Because…' And the Doctor paused. 'Actually, tell you what, pick a reason. I'm busy.' He stood there. He didn't look busy. He looked lost.

'Did a Custodian take them?'

'Not a helpful question,' the Doctor snapped. 'They're just killing. No. It's whatever that other creature was.'

'But that's also killing.'

'Yes, and leaving the bodies lying around. But it's also taking some of them. So maybe, maybe there's just the tiniest chance for her. For both her and

Bentley. But, just so's you know, it's mostly Clara I care about.'

'Me too.'

'Anyway –' his face twisted nastily – 'Bentley will be fine. She's got a superior attitude and a gun. That never fails.'

I coughed. 'Doctor, if I may… I preferred you when you were less ranty.'

'Believe me, I've shouted whole planets out of the skies.'

'But… this whole prison is tearing itself apart. And apparently the HomeWorld is too. Aren't there more important things? Than, er, than…'

'Do go on.' His tone was deadly.

'… Than the girl,' I finished feebly.

He spun round and only winced a little. 'No. And you know that, don't you?'

I did. I rather liked Clara. I nodded.

The Doctor smiled back at me. Just a little.

'I was just, well, saying…' I stammered a little. 'I was just saying the right thing.'

The Doctor held up a hand. 'Governor,' he said, 'Starting from now until all this is over, don't bother saying the right thing. Take your better nature out for a trot around the block. It needs the exercise.' He vanished back into the Control Station.

The Doctor surveyed the ruined Control Station and

then went over to the prison map.

'Something's hiding inside this prison – or rather, something's been hidden from you.' He waved a hand at the map. 'Now, you see… We take maps on trust. We have to, otherwise the world wouldn't work. We'd spend all day wondering if someone's cut a few corners on the coastline or left out some shops. But what if the map was part of the lie?'

I looked at the map of The Prison. It was so familiar to me. I knew every step of it. All six levels and conduits leading down to Level 7.

'Thing is,' said the Doctor, 'it's just a computer image. It's not real. If we want to find Clara and Bentley, we have to make it real. Luckily, you've got the most sensitive scanning equipment in the system here. The only problem is it's dedicated to scanning the skies for any approaching craft. Now, I'm going to turn it inwards, but to do that I need…'

The Doctor dived under the wreckage of a terminal.

'I need a shopping trolley,' he said, emerging.

'What?'

'Shopping trolley… shopping trolley… Marge Simpson,' he snapped, performing a mystical mime. 'Old dance move from the Astoria. I'm trying to tell you I really need to get my anti-grav trolley. Which is full of lovely things I stole from the workshop. Including a network hub controller.'

'What's one of those?'

'That's why I said "lovely things". I don't just do it for effect,' The Doctor beamed. 'Just bring me the lot. It'll save time. If I'm right, it's parked down on the stairs by Level 4. Can you pop down and get it for me?'

'Alone?'

'Alone.' The Doctor tugged at the cabling. 'I'm busy and immobile. And maybe, if you see any Custodians they'll leave you alone. After all, you are the Governor.'

'I think that's precisely why they will kill me.'

'Ah, well in that case, good luck.' With a grin, the Doctor vanished under the console.

'I, ah…'

'You've got ten minutes before the lack of a network hub controller irritates me,' he growled. 'Get going, Governor.'

'I have a name you know,' I said, a little hurt.

'Sure you do,' his voice muttered indistinctly, 'But it's a little late for learning new facts now, isn't it?'

I left him to it and found the staircase. In case you're wondering, I didn't feel at all happy about this. I didn't have a gun. I didn't have anything. Just a really nervous expression. I got the feeling the Doctor and Clara ran up and down corridors all the time. But I just felt very alone and frightened.

In theory it was very straightforward. Just go down four flights of stairs, and collect the Doctor's trolley. But the lights had gone in the stairwell. I made do by toggling the light on my communications blipper as a torch. It would shine for five seconds and then go off. I could see where I was going. I could pick my way over the bodies.

From time to time the asteroid shook and lurched. The Defence Array was still pounding away at the surface of the rock. We were fairly solid, but even so, at some point there would be an explosive decompression. And maybe that would be it. Maybe all my worries would be over when I was sucked screaming out into space. I'd never have to worry about everything I'd got wrong in my life ever again. I could just enjoy a little peace.

I smiled at that.

My comm blipped. At first I could hear breathing. I nearly spoke back to it, but an instinct stilled me. I could just hear breathing and another noise. A steady clicking. Then a voice. It was Bentley's. She sounded in great pain.

'Please… let me go… take her…'

'Thanks.'

Well, that was Clara accounted for.

'Why are you doing this? What can you want with us?'

More dragging.

'Yeah,' Clara again. 'I'm just a tourist, and Tin Knickers here doesn't strike me as cooperative.'

More dragging.

Bentley spoke again. 'Where are you taking us? You've brought us all the way down here.'

'Yes.' Clara sounded wooden. 'I mean, where are we now, would you say?'

'Well,' began Bentley. 'We're on Lev—' She cried out in sudden pain and then the comm terminated.

Shaken, I moved on further down the staircase.

And then I heard it. The gliding noise. I was on Level 3. Just one more flight of stairs to go. But the stairwell was hopelessly blocked by rubble. And, just beyond the door was the unmistakeable sound of a Custodian, gliding forwards and backwards. Waiting for me.

Clara would have charmed it. The Doctor would have shouted at it. My arsenal was rather more limited. Perhaps it would obey me – well, so the Doctor thought. Fat chance. Nothing around here had ever really obeyed me. Sweating, I crouched still in the darkness. The Custodian beyond the door showed no signs of moving away. Had it sensed me? Possibly.

I crawled back up the steps, feeling my way among the bodies, trying to see if there was anything useful in their clothes. I felt a terrible sense of revulsion at this. I'd let these people die and now I was going through their pockets. It was fairly fruitless. I found a bunch of keys, which seemed ironic.

I made my way back down the steps, thought

things through, and then, a couple of moments later, I stepped behind the staircase door and flung it open.

The Custodian glided onto the landing, illuminating the damaged staircase with the light on its fascia. It swivelled left and right, trying to locate me. Its antennae were out and snapping lethally. I threw the bunch of keys off to the left and the Custodian fired a blast as it rolled towards them. As it did so, I smashed a lump of rubble into the back of its head near the recharge port, and then another, breaking the light.

The Custodian ground back and forth, disoriented. I darted to the left, snatched up the keys and ran out of the door, closing it behind me. I fitted a key to the lock. It didn't work. I tried another one. The fourth one worked. Sort of.

The corridor filled with the metallic clank of the Custodian grinding against the stairwell door. There'd be no way back through there. And probably more Custodians on their way.

My comm panel blipped.

It was Clara, whispering.

'Hey you,' she said. She was sounding very casual.

'Where are you?'

'I really don't know,' she said. 'But you wouldn't like it. Is the Doctor with you?'

'No. I'm getting some things for him. He's trying to find where you are.'

'Right. No idea. After the last go, it knocked us out.'

'What did?'

'I'm going to say I haven't a clue, because if I tried telling you, you really wouldn't like it.'

'Right. Are you scared?'

There was a pause.

'Yes,' Clara replied. 'Please get a move on.'

'I will do,' I said. 'If something's been hiding in my prison then I... well, I need to...'

'I'm fairly certain it's broken a few rules. You can give it a lecture.'

'Thanks. Stay safe.' I said.

'Uh-huh. Get the Doctor. Hurry.' Clara ended the conversation.

While we'd been talking, I'd been making my way down to Level 4 using the gangways in the Prisoner Accommodation.

The whole cell area was eerie and unsettled. It had never seemed a cheery place, but now, empty, the Prison seemed terrifyingly dead. It had been designed to be a cramped space, full of life. It was now utterly lacking even the menacing patrol of Custodians.

My feet echoed against the metal stairs like thunderclaps, but somehow I made it down to Level 4.

The Doctor's trolley was wedging open a door. There'd clearly been a firefight in the corridor between Custodians and Guardians. One Custodian lay on its side, case cracked, antennae twitching weakly. Several more Guardians were in crumpled heaps along the wall. It didn't look as though the Guardians had won the battle.

In the darkness beyond the doorway, an ominous gliding was coming closer. I had to hurry.

The trolley was too damaged to move. Realising there was no way I could drag the trolley back to the Control Station, I filled my pockets with the assortment of junk, hoping one of them was the network hub controller. I made my way as quickly as I could back up to the Doctor.

The Control Station was even more of a mess. Half the TransNet room had been pulled out and patched into the terminal the Doctor was wedged under.

I dumped the components in a rattling heap on the floor.

'Doctor, I—'

A hand shot out from under the console, grabbed a lump of metal, waved it around and then threw it away. The hand grabbled on among the junk.

'Doctor, listen, Clara and Bentley, they're alive – they called me—'

'Network hub controller!' The Doctor sprung up from underneath the desk, holding one of the items I'd brought. He hastily wired it in between the TransNet system and the terminal he'd been working on. 'Thing about your TransNet hook-up is that it's rubbish at conveying a signal all the way to the HomeWorld. But it should be pretty good at using the local Sensor Array. I just need to get the sensors to look inwards instead of outwards and… and…'

There was a loud *thunk* from the terminal he'd been working on. The illuminated prison map went dark.

I looked at the Doctor. 'Clara said they're in a lot of trouble.'

'Of course she would. They are.' The Doctor continued to stare at the blank screen. 'Come on… come on… come on…'

It flickered.

'UPDATING… UPDATING…'

The Doctor made hopeful motions.

The screen refreshed again.

'Currently installing update 1 of 83. Please do not turn this terminal off during this process.'

The Doctor gave a howl of frustration. I thought about saying something, but he silenced me with a glare.

'It's not a delay,' he muttered to himself. 'It's a really good chance to work out what I'm going to do next.'

The prison map sprang into life – a picture of the whole asteroid, the detail gradually filling out as the Sensor Array finished its sweep.

The Doctor gave a roar of triumph. 'Can you see that?'

At first glance it looked pretty much the same to me.

'Oh, brilliant!' cried the Doctor, 'On the way here, I was counting the steps. Between Level 7 and Level 5… I noticed there were a few more steps – a bit more space between levels.' He jabbed a finger at a shady area of the map I'd not noticed before.

'It may just be barrier shielding,' I suggested.

'Barrier shielding against what?'

'I don't know,' I said. 'Solar radiation?'

'Piffle.' The Doctor pointed at the map jubilantly. That shaded area was gradually clearing as the Sensor Array finished its sweep. It showed a chamber in between Levels 5 and 6.

'What is that?'

The Doctor didn't answer. He was already lurching towards the door. 'When you went down to Level 6 you found it empty, didn't you?' He snatched up a semi-functioning tablet which he appeared to have stuck together with tape. 'It's where you put the prisoners you wanted to forget about. Which means that you wouldn't notice if it was being gradually emptied…'

'What?'

'The cells had been tidied, all trace of their occupants removed. They'd been empty for some time.' The Doctor held up the tablet, waving around a vast array of spreadsheets I'm fairly certain he shouldn't have been able to access. 'I told you to check the logs. These are the dates on which power fluctuations occurred. And this graph shows the dates when hopeless cases were transferred down to Level 6. They match pretty closely, don't they?'

We got to the stairwell, and he started limping as fast as he could down it. His eyes glinted in the dark. 'I'm very much afraid you've been feeding something for a long time.'

'And that's what's got Clara?'

The Doctor nodded. 'Something very hungry.'

Infuriatingly, we didn't go straight to Level 6. Instead the Doctor led us to the medical wing. Abesse was stood by the door, guarding it with a rifle. She saluted when I appeared.

'Good of you to show up, Governor,' she said drily. She hefted up the gun. 'I took this from a fleeing Guardian. Power-pack fully charged. He'd not even tried firing it. He just ran straight into the arms of a Custodian, so he didn't get far.'

'Well, then, I'm pleased you're alive, 203. Er... Abesse.'

Abesse saluted the Doctor, a little less sarcastically. 'I've followed your instructions, sir,' she said to him. *SIR?*

'Your instructions?' I boggled.

The Doctor acknowledged the salute. 'Thank you,

Major. Where's the patient?'

Abesse led us to the back of the sick bay.

'I thought you didn't like people with guns?' I said.

'I'm flexible in a crisis,' he admitted. 'And anyway…
Abesse is good people. She thinks before she shoots.'

'She's a mercenary,' I hissed.

Abesse heard me. She turned and smiled
dangerously at both of us. 'Tell me more,' she said.

'Yes,' continued the Doctor, 'Abesse is a mercenary.
Which means that she has no agenda other than
wanting to live.'

'True,' said Abesse, and raised her gun towards me.
I tried not to flinch, and failed. 'Well, perhaps a tiny
agenda,' she admitted, and lowered the gun.

Abesse pulled back a curtain. Behind it, slumped
in her chair, was Marianne Globus, fast asleep. Poor
Marianne.

'She's sedated,' announced Abesse. 'I presume
you'd like her waking?'

The Doctor considered the slumbering form.
'When she's awake, she's in agony, isn't she?' His voice
could be very gentle sometimes.

Abesse nodded. 'Her condition is getting worse.'

The Doctor stepped forward. 'Well then, let's not
wake her,' he whispered. 'I'll just try and talk to her
telepathically.'

As though people said that all the time.

Abesse shot him an uncertain look. The same look

I'd worn since I'd first met Prisoner 428. Were any of us right to trust him?

His hand rested softly on an unblemished area of Marianne's forehead and his eyes closed in deep contemplation. He let out a long, steady breath. Somewhere, a long way away, lost in a hopefully dreamless sleep, Marianne stirred. Her hand twitched slightly. Her dribbling mouth made a tiny murmur.

The Doctor nodded to himself and then closed his eyes. A muscle in the side of his cheek twitched. Apart from that, the rest of him was still.

The Doctor spoke.

'You're all the way over there, Marianne. It's all right. You can stay there. If you want to. It's fine. Between you and me there's a lot of pain. Some of it mine, I will admit. Most of it yours. It's all right. You don't have to cross it. I'll come to you. No, don't worry. It's fine. I'll bring biscuits.'

The slight twitch in his cheek became more pronounced. He let out another deep breath, ragged as the edge of saw. All the time, the Doctor's voice, soothing and delicate continued. I noticed his lips weren't moving.

'Do you mind if I join you? There seems enough room for two over there. Yes. So. Hello. We've not been properly introduced have we? You're the famous Marianne Globus. Well, I'm the Doctor. Pleased to meet you. It's been a while since you've had a visitor, hasn't it? Well, then, let's do all the gossip shall we? Let me see—

'No, no, it's all right. There's no need to cry. There's no need. It's all right. Come here. This isn't really a huggy body, but what's the harm, just once, eh? There now. It's fine, Marianne. What happened to you was bad. But no one's fault. It was an accident. You didn't deserve it. No, no matter what you did. Listen – we all do bad things. But we also do good things. And that's the fun stuff. Always think about the bacon sandwich and not the washing-up.'

He frowned again. 'Oh… oh I see. Really? I'm so sorry. I'll get back to that. No. It's a promise. I will deal with it. So, yes. Of course I'm here because I need your help. I know I said I'd brought biscuits, but that was just me using my charm. Oh, shut up. I do have charm. This is me doing charming. It just gets mistaken for indigestion. Normally by Clara.

'Let me tell you about Clara. She's one that's worth saving. Once I got so lost she walked the universe looking for me. So, the least I can do is find her in a cold lump of space rock. And I need your help for that. Because of what's down there. You've seen it. You've survived it. Which makes you amazing and very important. So I'm wondering if you'll come with me? Sounds like we've both got a score to settle.

'You will? Brilliant! Come on then, Marianne Globus, let's get out of here.'

He gently took hold of the back of her chair, where Marianne met the base of a Custodian, and set off.

If I'd ever fooled myself that I was in command of The Prison, well, I really wasn't now. I was just tailing behind this strange man, pushing all that remained of a once good friend of mine, the two of them guarded over by Abesse. The mercenary with a really big gun she was just itching to use. I didn't even have a gun. I know the Doctor said he didn't approve of them, but perhaps if I had one, then I could have helped. Even though I'd never fired a gun.

We made it down a level before the Custodians came for us. They waited until we reached a hallway. Walls on every side. They emerged, gliding from docking ports, surrounding us.

Abesse started firing.

The Doctor was shouting at her, telling her not to. But she was a trained mercenary. Mercenaries sometimes act purely on finely honed instinct. Her bullets rammed into the carapaces of the machines. They juddered but kept on coming.

The Doctor was launching into a speech about it being a waste of bullets, not that all bullets weren't a waste or something. You know, sometimes, he could be a bit monotonous. When I ruled the HomeWorld System, you'd get people like that coming in to see you from time to time. Open Government. You'd dodge most of the meetings, but it looked good to see the odd crank. Funny that. If I'd met the Doctor in real life, I'd have run a mile. But suddenly, right here, trapped in a dying space prison surrounded by lethal robots, he seemed quite the best person to be standing next to. Even if he did like the sound of his own voice.

The Custodians moved towards us, gliding and bumping, the bullets whizzing off their bodies. Their antennae were out, claws and pincers snapping, blasters charging. The air crackled dangerously. They'd electrified their casings.

I looked at poor Marianne, lost in distant dreams in her chair. She was almost smiling. For once, she wouldn't feel a thing. Not when the end came. That seemed a good thing. Poor Marianne. I'm so sorry.

The Custodians closed in.

What happened next was a bit of a surprise.

We will ignore Abesse catching me in the shoulder with a stray blast. She really didn't mean to, and anyway, it was more of a flesh wound. It was simply that she didn't expect me to suddenly walk forward and stand in front of her gun. Between her and the Custodians.

The Doctor was staring at me in horror. I didn't need telepathy to know he thought this was a very stupid thing to do.

I stood there. Between my... my friends and the Custodians.

'Custodians,' I said. 'What are your orders?'

The Custodians don't, as a habit, speak. Some units had various simple vocabulary banks.

'Halt,' said the one in front of me.

'Halt? Halt me? I am your Governor.'

'Halt. Prisoners. Stop.'

'Stop all of us?'

'Command. Halt. Prisoners.'

'You think we're all prisoners? Is that it?'

I was painfully aware of how close the Custodian was to me. The air around it stank with electricity. The hairs on the back of my neck stood up. It was still coming towards me. Slowly.

'Prisoners. Halt.'

'I am not a prisoner. I say again, I am your Governor. I order you to halt.'

'Priority Command. Governor Protocol not recognised.'

The thing is, life sometimes offers you clarity. I'd got a lot wrong. But as the Doctor said, everyone must get something right occasionally, too. Sometimes.

'Define your Priority Command.'

'Priority: Once cascade systems failure initiated, the definition of Prisoner is extended to all life forms in The Prison. All Prisoners are to be restrained with lethal force. That is Emergency Protocol.'

The Custodian glided a little closer.

Abesse pulled up her gun, ready to fire again.

The Doctor's hand was on my shoulder, ready to pull me back.

The Custodian was now so close the field around it tugged at the skin on my arms.

'Emergency Protocol is superseded in one case,' I said. I gestured to the people behind me. 'This is a Medical Evacuation. She –' I gestured to Marianne – 'is a critically ill patient. Scan her. I and Abesse here are her two guardians, and this –' I tapped the Doctor – 'is her appointed physician. That's a squad of four. As per the Protocols.'

The Custodian checked this. 'Medical Evacuation is superseded—'

'No,' I insisted. 'Isn't that right, Doctor?'

'Yes.' The Doctor suddenly sounded very sure of himself. 'Medical Evacuation is also an Emergency Protocol.' He nodded emphatically. I wondered how – when – he'd read the manual. He just winked at me and suddenly that felt enormously encouraging.

'And,' I continued, 'since this Medical Evacuation was already enacted before your Emergency Protocols, then it cannot be superseded. It's a Prior Operation.'

The Custodians surveyed us. 'Where is the Medical Evacuation taking place?' the lead one asked.

'We are removing this prisoner to Level 6. To…' I faltered.

'To the Secure Area,' finished the Doctor approvingly.

'Once Medical Evacuation is completed, then Termination Protocol will be activated,' the Custodian informed us.

'Yes, yes, of course.' The Doctor sounded only a little testy. 'Once we've saved her, then by all means kill us all. Perhaps, you know,' he leant forward confidentially to the Custodian, 'if you conveyed us directly to the Secure Area, then we could pick up the pace, eh?'

The Custodians conferred and then agreed.

And so, unbelievably, the Custodians acted as our escort to the Secure Area. It had been hidden from the entire prison population, but the Custodians had known where it was all the time. You just had to ask.

'Machine logic,' chuckled the Doctor, 'Never fails.'

'You have mobility issues?' A Custodian had noticed the Doctor hobbling. Antennae shot out of it.

'It's just a toe, it's fine,' he reassured it. 'There's no need to execute me now. If you did so, my patient's health would suffer.'

The Custodian considered this, but also remained fascinated by the Doctor's toe. 'Your progress is impeding the Priority Medical Evacuation.' It moved backwards. 'Stay there.'

'What are you going to do?' the Doctor demanded. 'Don't think you can dispose of me and order a

224

replacement. There aren't any other medics on The Prison. You've killed them all So, you'll just have to put up with me hobbling a little. It's not too bad.'

The Custodian considered.

'Just a little delay,' repeated the Doctor, gesturing towards the stairs. 'Shall we?'

The Custodian considered. And then shot the Doctor in the foot.

He screamed and fell to the floor.

'Now you are injured enough for us to carry you,' announced the Custodian smugly, and picked the Doctor up. A lift opened. 'Efficiency improved.'

'Machine logic,' I couldn't resist saying to the Doctor. 'Never fails.'

You can tell a lot about a building by taking a journey in a lift.

The lifts in HomeWorld Parliament were impressive glass boxes designed to create a sense of awe.

The lift through The Prison was for emergency freight transportation only. A dull grey box. Prisoners and Guardians could use the stairs. Only Custodians had the pass key to the lift. Hindsight's an interesting thing – it told you who'd really been in charge here all along.

I looked at my fellow passengers. They really didn't tell me much. The Custodians were impassive. Marianne was asleep. Abesse looked straight ahead, and actually, I didn't really fancy looking the Doctor in the eye.

Instead I watched the floor indicator lights crawl by. We were on Level 4. Level 6 was the bottom. Beneath that was a light for the Level 7 docking bay. We reached Level 6. And halted. Then the Custodian's claw extended into a socket and, with a tiny judder, the lift shook and moved further down.

Now it was impossible to ignore the look on the Doctor's face. It was triumph. Triumph and 'I told you so', mixed, just a little, with 'I've been shot'. I'd never really considered that there were more steps down to Level 7. It had always seemed appropriate that it was a tiny bit further away. It wasn't really part of my job to wonder about it. Don't think too hard. That wasn't my job.

The lift scraped and juddered to a halt. And then the doors opened.

We walked out into a space that shouldn't exist.

'Oh my,' said the Doctor.

13

The thing about the Blood Cell was just how wrong it all was.

The easy thing to describe was the room's shape. It was a large cube hewn out of the rock. What had happened to it after that was as though a madman had been told to go enjoy himself.

The simple wrongness of the room was that it was. I'll try again.

Everything happened at once. Everything sort of happened. Everyone moved. Everyone stood still.

I can tell you that the Custodians glided from the lift to stand either side of us. As an escort, they looked absurdly like a wedding arch. The last time I'd been through one, my friends had been standing on either side of me, grinning wildly, and I'd been walking hand in hand with Helen. There'd been confetti. It had been the happiest day of my life.

Now I was travelling through a barricade of lethal robots. I was in procession with a trained killer, a comatose ex-friend, and behind us came the Doctor, carried wriggling in the arms of a Custodian.

The whole situation, the whole sight of the Blood Cell was such that the Doctor somehow did two things simultaneously. Looking back, I'm not sure how this can have happened.

On the one hand, he shouted out Clara's name.

On the other hand, as we came gliding through that dreadful arch of robots, he hummed 'The Entry Of The Toreadors' from *Carmen*. You know, *tum-tum-ti-tum-tum, tum-ti-tum-ti-tum*…

I would have laughed, only the Blood Cell was… No. I still can't quite describe it.

You could tell, right then, that the Doctor had been to places like this before, places that exist only in nightmares.

One thing. Abesse, who had led several battles, swore and turned away, revolted. I'm not sure that that helped her. The smell, that rich, metallic smell, it clogged the air.

My brain kept returning to it. Trying to step around it or through it.

Tiptoe past the sleeping giant.
Fee fi fo fum. I smell the blood
No no no.
Start again.

This is getting us nowhere. I've managed fine so far.

I've told you the story. I've not spared myself. I've told the truth. Even when notes that I've written earlier have made me out to be an idiot or a liar. I've done my best. But something about the Blood Cell. About how it could have happened.

The best way to approach it is to look at it another way. The whole room had been decorated and filled not by a madman, not even by a man. By something that sought to understand a man.

Perhaps, once you appreciate that what had happened there had been done by a machine, it might make more sense.

The Doctor later told me of a race of clockwork robots that viewed people as little more than a source of inferior spare parts. He also told me of a race of living silver suits of armour who viewed the people inside them as little more than a bad start. The Doctor talked, and these things all sounded like fairy stories. Fairy stories you'd tell particularly badly behaved children.

The room had been filed.
The Prison had been filed.
There was a reason the bodies of the Guardians had been left behind. There was no use for them. The owner of the Blood Cell had been happy to leave them to be wiped out by the Custodians. It had only been

interested in the prisoners.

Survivors are an odd thing. A handful of pages ago, I was delighted for the prisoners who'd managed to escape on Level 7. Then I was distraught when Level 7 was blown up. Then I was happy to learn that they'd survived.

Over a hundred prisoners had been left behind on The Prison. Once I'd regretted they'd been left behind, then been glad for them, then worried about the lingering fate that awaited them. Now it was too late. They'd all come here. Where they'd been processed. My latest failure.

When an inmate arrives at The Prison, they are entered into the system. It is a ritual. It serves the useful purpose of telling them that we are in charge. We take away their clothes, we take away their personal effects. We give them clothes and a number. We have logged and filed and sorted them.

The same thing had happened here in the Blood Cell. The remaining prisoners had been processed.

'Processed' is a good word. Logged and filed and sorted. Entered into a system. These are all reasonable phrases. When you are talking about objects and clothing. But not about bodies.

A fair amount of each prisoner had been taken away. And placed… placed into piles.

I hope you're squeamish. I know I am. So I shan't describe it any further than that. Unless I have to.

This is no fairy tale for naughty children.

There were three other things in the room. Bentley seemed fine. Clara seemed terrified. And then there was the creature itself.

It was the same thing that we'd encountered twice before. The thing that had attacked Lafcardio. The creature that had come for us on Level 6. But it was much bigger now.

It was basically a Custodian. In the same way you could argue that Marianne was basically a Custodian because her wheelchair was made out of one. But this was a very large Custodian. Previously it had been shrouded in plastic sheeting. Most of that was now gone. The bits that remained were splattered like a butcher's apron.

This Custodian had grown. It had stolen several other Custodians and augmented itself from them, making itself considerably larger. But it hadn't stopped at Custodians.

At first the Creature didn't acknowledge us, simply moving between various unmentionable piles. Sorting. Adding to itself. Discarding.

'Revolting isn't it?' called Clara.

'Clara,' the Doctor waved weakly, 'Are you all right?'

'Yeah,' she said.

She clearly wasn't. She was fastened to a grimly

stained bench and she was clearly terrified. 'It's ignored us so far. What about you? You got a robot nanny to carry you about now? Seriously? Because of your hurty toe?'

The Doctor wriggled in the Custodian's arms. 'Actually, my foot got shot.'

'The same foot?' Clara clucked, trying to seem casual and not at all terrified. 'Unlucky.'

The Doctor didn't answer her. He was surveying the room, making sense of it. The large creature. The piles of neatly sorted objects. Clara and Bentley's benches were raised a little off the ground. Near a revolting-smelling drain cover.

I went over to Clara. The creature didn't try and stop me.

'I am sorry about this,' I said to her. 'No one should have to see this.'

'It's OK,' Clara said. 'I think my brain took one look and shut down. It'll be a while before I dare have dreams.'

'I had no idea this was here,' I assured her. 'I mean, really. None at all.'

Clara laughed. It sounded horrid in this room. 'There was an abattoir in your prison, and you didn't notice? You really are a total failure of a Governor.'

I nodded. 'I'm not going to argue with you.' I looked over to the Doctor. 'What's he going to do?'

'Something,' said Clara. 'Hopefully.'

The Doctor continued to lie in the Custodian's arms. Looking around the room. Thinking.

Bentley had woken up now as well, and was also staring at the Doctor. 'Come on!' she yelled. 'Get us out of here.'

The Doctor shook his head. 'I need to work out what to do.'

'I'll tell you what to do,' Bentley shouted. 'You don't stand around thinking. You take action. You do something.'

The Doctor twisted his head to one side trying to see more of the room. Then he motioned to his Custodian and whispered, 'Gee up!' It glided towards Bentley, bringing him to her.

Bentley was shouting now. Terror and panic had driven her to hysteria. In her rage, she was holding the Doctor responsible for everything in The Prison, for the deaths of her Guardians, for Level 7, for everything on the HomeWorld, for the plague, for the steady collapse of the System.

'It's all happened,' she was babbling, 'because you wouldn't do the right thing. No one would.'

The Doctor had reached Bentley. Draped in the Custodian's arms, he was level with her face.

'Tell me one thing,' said the Doctor. 'Why has this creature kept you alive? It didn't need any of the other Guardians. It didn't even need poor Lafcardio.

Because they were innocent. But it kept you. Didn't it?'

Bentley glared at him with mute rage.

'You want me to do something?' The Doctor gave his full attention to Bentley. 'Because I'll tell you something. I've worked out what to do. But I don't like any of it. You know what's been nice about being in this Prison? I've not had to make any tough decisions. Not for a long time. It's been peaceful. I've spent every day of the last few thousand years waking up wondering if I could have done things better. But for the last few weeks I've not had to do that. I've just had to worry about how bad breakfast was. But every holiday has to come to an end.' The Doctor let out a long sigh that filled the room. 'So I'll tell you what – I'll go and do something.'

The Doctor tugged at the Custodian and it glided away. Bentley watched him go.

It was still impressive.

The Doctor looked at the Creature. The Creature continued sifting through its various piles.

'I don't know,' continued the Doctor. 'What should I call it?'

The Custodian carrying the Doctor spoke up. 'It is called the Judge.'

'Really?' The Doctor continued to watch the creature glide across to a filing cabinet. It opened a drawer, took something awful out, and hung it onto itself. It shut the drawer and then glided away.

'The Judge,' the Doctor repeated. 'And what is it for?'

'It does not yet know,' the Custodian said, and then shut up, seemingly refusing to answer further questions.

The Doctor continued to regard The Judge. 'Can you talk?' he asked it. 'I would like to talk with you.'

The Judge paused. It seemed to notice the Doctor, cradled in the Custodian's arms.

Please remember – Bentley had demanded the Doctor do something. Just remember that. In some way it was her fault. She'd brought it on herself. She'd deserved it. That's what I tell myself, when I remember what happened next.

The Judge reached casually across to Bentley, lifting her from her bench. And then it took her voice.

It simply plugged Bentley into itself. There was, after all, plenty of room on it. And she fitted. More or less. Sort of. With only a little cramming. Tentacles and tendrils wrapped themselves around her wetly and squeezed. And then, after one scream and a long and terrible silence, Bentley spoke to the Doctor.

'I recognise you,' it croaked. 'You are more than these others. You wished to speak with me? Speak.'

The Doctor swallowed. 'I'm not sure…' he said, and his voice was dry, 'that after all that, it was really worth it.'

Bentley's empty head regarded him with what might have been bitter irony. 'I repeat,' said the Judge through her throat. 'You wished to speak to me.'

'What are you for?' said the Doctor.

The Judge paused. 'I do not know. My function confuses me. I was built as the final weapon. To wipe out any remaining population in The Prison.' Bentley's dead brow pulled down in a mockery of a frown. 'But that seems unnecessary. There are already enough ways for the prisoners to die. I was redundant. That cannot be right.' Bentley's lips pulled back and air hissed out in a ghastly attempt at a sigh. 'That cannot be right.'

The Doctor nudged his Custodian, and they glided up to the Judge. 'You don't know much about humans, do you? Some of them like making really sure that people die.'

'You are correct,' admitted the Judge. 'I do not know enough about people. So I set about to learn. When the systems failures activated me, I became curious. I was called the Judge. A judge assesses the merit of humans. That is what I am doing.'

'By wearing bits of them as jewellery?' The Doctor raised an eyebrow. Bentley's face followed suit.

'The population of the System is being destroyed by plague. I sought permission from HomeWorld to carry out investigations into the cause of the plague.

Under the terms of their captivity, Prisoners do not need to give their consent to take part in clinical trials.'

Struggling in the grip of his Custodian, the Doctor flung an arm out at the neat, disgusting piles around him. 'This is a clinical trial?'

The Judge was unruffled. 'It was a commonly held belief that illness is caused by sin. I am seeking to see if that is so. I am searching their bodies for the cure. I am assessing each guilty prisoner and finding the source of their sins.' It indicated the gruesome trophies dangling from it. 'Then I wear them. So that I understand them.'

The Doctor stared at the Judge for a long time. He looked about to say something several times. Then didn't.

'From the sample I have made,' the Judge continued, 'there are so many different things that humans do to each other and their reasons are so complicated and conflicting. People who do wrong because they think it is right, or because they want to help. People who hurt those they love. By studying the sins of the prisoners, I have learned so much about humans.'

'They're complicated, aren't they? The thing you've missed is—' The Doctor began a speech, but the Judge talked over him.

'I have learned so much. But not enough. I must build up a complete picture.'

'Does it mean us?' I hissed at the Doctor.

'Oh, if only it did,' he muttered. 'I think it's not only given itself a purpose in life. It's going on a crusade.'

The Judge leaned over the Doctor, Bentley's head flopping forward, wearing a ghastly grin.

'You interest me,' it informed him. 'You have recognised the failings of your self. You have augmented yourself into that machine as I have absorbed so many into myself. You understand.'

The Doctor started to say that he didn't, but the Judge spoke over him again.

'I must finish my study. I need to expand my sample. In order to do that, I think must leave here. And you will help me.' The Judge leaned back and indicated Clara. 'Or,' it said, 'I shall be forced to assess the soul of this one here.'

'You can't!' yelled the Doctor. 'She's an outsider. An innocent.'

'Quite,' Bentley's head pulled itself into that same awful smile. 'It will provide a useful contrast to the other specimens. Where better to begin?'

The Doctor writhed in the grip of his Custodian. I felt utterly powerless.

Occasionally, within the mesh of tendrils, bits of Bentley would thrash, which made me wonder if she was quite dead. I hoped she was. I'd never really liked her, but even she didn't deserve this.

The Doctor twisted his head round to look at

me. 'So, Governor...' His voice was so low it was practically an icy breath. 'Here we have humanity.' With some difficulty, he gestured around the room. 'I don't know why I make the effort. Poverty? Disease? The hoovering? Ah, can't be bothered. But no, when it comes to being cruel to each other, and devising needlessly complicated weapons, oh my word, you're all over it. The result is this grotesque nightmare... Only humans could be so idiotic.'

'This, this isn't my fault!' I protested, but the Doctor was already sarcastically echoing my words.

'Not his fault! Hah!' He turned to jab a finger at the Judge. 'Did you hear that, Judge? Not his fault.'

The Judge leaned over Clara. Hands that were not originally its own grasped knives and scalpels.

The Doctor squirmed frantically in the robot restraining him. 'You know what, Clara, I lied. I'm very much afraid you're probably going to die, and it's my fault,' he said. He spoke so tenderly. 'Because I'm the idiot here. I thought these people were worth helping. But no, only humanity would build this obscenity.' He nodded towards the Judge. 'No offence – but you're awful. On a prison full of lethal traps, they added a redundant backup system that was so smart it figured it couldn't possibly just be a surplus weapon. Oh no. It set out to find the meaning of life. And how's that going?'

The Judge paused in its examination of Clara and

glanced towards the Doctor. 'A Judgement must be made.'

'Exactly.' The Doctor clapped slowly. 'Like an old Egyptian god, you've weighed up the souls of the guilty, lump by gristly lump, and still you've not got an answer. So you're going to spread out across the stars. All because you – are – utterly – pointless.' The Doctor punctuated his last sentence with a jab of his finger. 'And I can't let that happen.'

No one spoke. Eventually, the Judge moved. Bentley's mouth fell slackly open. 'I must know.'

'No, sunshine, you really mustn't.' The Doctor sounded so old and tired. 'They're really not worth the bother, Judge. You're stupid, I'm stupid, but humanity – they're the biggest fools of all.'

I wanted to argue with him, but the room, the Judge, the terror on Clara's face… they all stopped me.

'You're a monstrosity dreamt up by idiots,' snapped the Doctor.

'I am not a monster,' replied the Judge flatly through Bentley's empty mouth. 'I am seeking to become a balanced creation.'

The Doctor waved at the piles that crammed the corners of the room. 'And have your learned anything?'

'I have learnt much.' The Judge towered over the Doctor. 'I have learned about the sins that weigh people down. If I opened you up, what would I find you guilty of?'

'Trust me,' the Doctor said grimly, 'you don't want to bother with that.'

'One final time,' the Judge said, hands moving closer to Clara. Bentley's jaw was making a wet, clicking noise whenever it spoke. I really wished it would stop doing that. 'Or I dismantle your companion and then you.'

'She has a name, you know,' sighed the Doctor.

'Are names important? I would like to know.' Bentley's head flopped over him, empty and agape.

I strode forward. 'Me,' I said, amazed to hear my own voice. 'Judge me.'

The Judge twisted to one side, turning Bentley's sightless eyes on me. How odd, I realised. This was the first time she'd ever actually looked at me. She must really have hated me.

'You are beyond the remit of my inquiry,' it announced regretfully. 'You are a figure in authority. My construction prevents me from examining them. They are above suspicion.'

The Doctor laughed at this. 'You finally do something noble, Governor,' he told me, 'and discover that your friends back home have prevented you from doing even that. How wonderfully corrupt your system is.'

'I can fix it,' I said.

The Doctor shrugged. 'It's really too late for that,'

he said. 'The only way out of this is to do something horrid. Something I really didn't want to do.'

With a triumphant shrug, he slipped out of the arms of the Custodian and dragged himself over to stand by the sleeping figure of Marianne.

I felt a chill inside me.

It did not take Marianne long to wake up. Abesse tapered off her medication, and she twitched, her remaining eyelid fluttering, a thin moan of pain coming from her mouth.

The Judge ceased its interest in Clara and strode over to examine Marianne. It halted suddenly.

'You recognise her, don't you?' The Doctor turned to face it. 'You spared her on Level 6. You took everyone else, but you left her behind. Remember?'

'I… remember…' The Judge made the admission grudgingly.

'You remember too, don't you, Marianne?' The Doctor spoke soothingly.

The figure jerked up and awake in its chair, mewling piteously. 'It could have ended… my suffering. I followed it… I begged it… but it ignored me.'

'More than that, it went away,' the Doctor said. He turned to the Judge. 'Why?'

The Judge made no answer.

'Thought you'd dodge that one,' the Doctor nodded. 'Doesn't matter. I know. It's why you spoke to me. You thought I was joined to a Custodian. And you spared Marianne because you felt a kinship with her. Didn't you? She's a hybrid of Custodian and human. You saw her and you spared her. Because it's what you want to be.'

'She is a perfectly balanced creation,' the Judge announced.

There was a noise then. A terrible noise I never wanted to hear again. The sound of Marianne Globus laughing.

That did it. The Doctor stumbled closer to the Judge, drawing himself up. 'She's perfectly balanced? Well, what about you, Judge? Judge yourself. Tell me how balanced you are.'

The Judge considered the Doctor's command. For a moment I sort of hoped that would be it. That the Judge would just fall apart right then, in a heap of its own sins.

Instead it made a noise, and snatched the Doctor up, pulling him towards itself. Tendrils snaked out of it and grabbed the Doctor. It was going to tear him apart.

'Balanced?' The voice rasped around the room.

Marianne's chair twitched and she started to move towards the Judge, her face contorted with agony. 'Do you want to know what balanced feels like?'

The Judge took a step backwards, dragging the Doctor with him. 'You are a pattern.'

Marianne continued to glide forwards, her head swivelling from side to side. 'I made decisions. Terrible decisions. It was my job to. And people hated me. Bentley hated me. She lost her whole family on the colonies. That's why she told me how to escape. It was a trap she'd set up. Revenge. She did this to me.' A stump pointed at her body. 'She felt I deserved it. That's justice. When death came, I finally felt a tiny bit better. But they wouldn't let me die.'

She was moving really quickly now, the gliding incessant as she moved closer and closer to the Judge. As she moved, I heard a whining noise. The Judge was swaying, backing away, the Doctor twisting wildly in its grasp.

Marianne's voice was loud now. No longer lost in pain. It was strong with fury. 'Bentley did this to me. I think she was happy I survived. At first. And then she couldn't bear it either. And no one here had the guts to just let me die. Not even the Governor.'

'Marianne—' I protested.

'He never had any courage to do that kind of thing.' She sounded almost fond. 'Perhaps the only person here who does is the Doctor. But he would never admit it. Because he is the hero.'

The Doctor said nothing, just struggled in the Judge's grasp. I had to admit, he didn't look particularly heroic. Especially not when the Judge flung him aside and he landed in a pile of shredded prison uniforms.

Marianne carried on gliding across the Blood Cell. The whining noise was growing louder. The Judge moved back again, and then stopped. Standing against the wet wall of the cell. It had run out of room. And still Marianne moved on. Something was glowing in the remains of her hand.

I turned to Abesse, protesting. 'Stop her, stop her somehow!'

Abesse raised her gun and fired it repeatedly at the base of Marianne's chair. It should have stopped her. Only nothing happened.

It was at this point that Abesse realised the power-pack was gone from her gun.

I went cold.

'Marianne,' I cried out. 'Stop, please!'

Marianne's chair swivelled back, facing me for a moment. 'Governor,' she said. 'Remember. It's just the little people. They don't count.' And then she closed in on the Judge, the whining growing shriller and shriller.

'Go on,' she snarled. 'I'm your answer. Judge me. Judge. Me. Because I am guilty.'

The Judge cowered back, that huge figure recoiling from the tiny righteous, crumpled frame of Marianne.

I think I called out her name first.

Or maybe the power-pack exploded first.

Perhaps Marianne cried out.

Or whatever remained of Bentley did.

But when the explosion had finished, peace came to The Prison.

14

The Doctor was cooking dinner.

'I've got lasagne at home,' protested Clara.

'Don't care,' said the Doctor. 'Mine will be better.'

'Is that even lasagne?' Clara was dubious.

The Doctor regarded the saucepans carefully, 'Let's say it still has the potential to be.'

I sat on a table in the canteen. I didn't feel like eating.

After the explosion we were all still alive. We were about the only things left in The Prison still functioning. The Custodians had all shut down. All that remained of the Judge was a heap of mostly metal that none of us fancied going anywhere near.

Abesse looked surprised to be still alive. The Doctor hobbled up to her, and, to my amazement, pinched her on the cheek. She pinched him back. 'I told you,' he said to her, 'the less shooting you do, the greater the chance of making it out alive.'

'You did,' Abesse admitted. 'But… some instincts are hard to overcome.'

'Aren't they just?' The Doctor stepped back. 'For instance, despite all the evidence, I just can't give up liking you humans.'

And Abesse then did a remarkable thing. She smiled.

You don't want to know about the stuff that followed. It turns out the big things, such as stabilising the Prison systems, restoring some limited life support and regaining control of the Defence Array, were relatively dull procedures. They all just took a little time. That was all. Not really worth talking about.

Eventually, the Doctor, the man who had once been Prisoner 428, stood up from the control panel he'd been re-routing and rubbed his eyes. 'That's that, then. I'm hungry,' he announced, and limped off.

Abesse didn't join us for dinner. She was trying to get the TransNet connection working again. She couldn't wait to see the look on the faces of the people on the other end. Especially when she told them that The Prison was now under the control of Prisoner 203. The outlawed mercenary Major Abesse, with all of The Prison's files at her fingertips.

So dinner was just the Doctor, me, and Clara.

'I'm not hungry,' I insisted.

'I don't care,' said the Doctor, chopping vegetables. 'This isn't about you. It was on my list. "Do something about the food." Hence this.'

'Oh,' Clara sighed. 'Of course. It's all about the lists with you.' She tried reaching over with a spoon into the Doctor's saucepan but he slapped her wrist away, 'Not yet,' he said. 'It's not ready.'

'Have you even decided what it it'll be?'

The Doctor shrugged and carried on cooking.

There was a rose in a plant pot on the table. It was covered in buds. They'd flower soon.

I'm still not sure what dinner was. But it was very nice. I started off eating a little of it, and then cleaned my bowl. And had another.

Clara looked at me expectantly. 'It's the paprika, isn't it? I told him to put that in.'

'I would,' the Doctor muttered, 'have put some in anyway.'

'Of course you would,' Clara said with a tight smile, and winked at me.

The Doctor pushed his bowl back. 'And now for dessert,' he announced.

'I don't have room!' I insisted.

'Oh, it's not a pudding, it's a decision. Your just dessert.'

Clara wrinkled her nose. I just felt dinner turn to lead somewhere in my stomach.

'What?' I said.

'Well…' The Doctor examined his fork, counting the tines on it over and over, 'Back home, the HomeWorld Government is falling. It's a terrible mess. A really terrible mess. Thing is, the people want you back.'

'I can't,' I said, 'I don't deserve to—'

'Oh, I know you don't.' The Doctor's voice was cold. 'But the people down there, they think you do. They've forgotten all the stupid human things you did, and all they can remember is that you were better than the new lot. A bit. And luckily for you –' he gestured around at the empty canteen – 'a lot of the people who can tell them otherwise are gone.'

'I had… nothing to do with…'

'Stop that.' The Doctor jabbed me in my injured shoulder with his fork. I shut up. 'I don't care. I don't go around being a kingmaker. It's not for me to overrule the will of the people. They think you're the best of a bad lot. More than that. They're on their way to declaring you a hero.'

I felt sick. I thought about all I'd done. All that had happened. All that I was responsible for. All that I wasn't. How much I missed being in power. How much I missed my Helen. How much I missed being happy.

'I don't know what to say,' I told him truthfully.

The Doctor leaned back and folded his arms. 'It's up to you,' he announced.

Clara spoke up. 'You don't have to go, you know.' She was smiling at me kindly. 'We can drop you off somewhere new. You never have to go back. And you don't have to make up your mind now. Take all the time you need. We've got some washing-up to do – and you wouldn't believe how long the Doctor takes over that.'

They stood up and went into the kitchen and spent some time bickering over the right way to wash dishes. It seemed absurd. Cleaning plates that would never be eaten from again. But then, the Doctor had said something about how these things always needed to be done properly.

I sat there and I thought about what they'd said. I looked around at the walls of the canteen, painted just the right colour. I looked at the rose. I rested my hands on the bench that the Doctor had made from burnt shelves, and then I rested my head on the bench. It felt cool.

'Well?' the Doctor was back, standing over me, holding a tea towel decorated, absurdly, with Old Earth cathedrals.

'What?' I said.

'What's it to be, Governor?' asked Prisoner 428. 'What decision have you made?'

I started off by writing this down. By finishing the journal I've been keeping. By reading it through. By making sure it's as full and honest and open as it can be. For when it's read. Whatever I choose, I want people to know. That's all.

I said before that there's one thing you learn in this job. It isn't what you say that tells you most about someone. It's your silence.

And, while I worked it all out, I said nothing.

But I've finished now. And the Doctor and Clara are still waiting to hear my answer.

Because it's time I made my mind up.

BBC
DOCTOR WHO

Silhouette

JUSTIN RICHARDS

ISBN 978-0-8041-4088-1

'*Vastra and Strax and Jenny? Oh no, we don't need to bother them. Trust me.*'

Marlowe Hapworth is found dead in his locked study, killed by an unknown assailant. This is a case for the Great Detective, Madame Vastra.

Rick Bellamy, bare-knuckle boxer, has the life drawn out of him by a figure dressed as an undertaker. This angers Strax the Sontaran.

The Carnival of Curiosities, a collection of bizarre and fascinating sideshows and performers. This is where Jenny Flint looks for answers.

How are these things connected? And what does Orestes Milton, rich industrialist, have to do with it all? As the Doctor and Clara join the hunt for the truth, they find themselves thrust into a world where nothing and no one are what they seem.

An original novel featuring the Twelfth Doctor and Clara, as played by Peter Capaldi and Jenna Coleman

BBC

DOCTOR WHO

The Crawling Terror

MIKE TUCKER

ISBN 978-0-8041-4090-4

'Well, I doubt you'll ever see a bigger insect.'

Gabby Nichols is putting her son to bed when she hears her daughter cry out. 'Mummy, there's a daddy longlegs in my room!' Then the screaming starts… Kevin Alperton is on his way to school when he is attacked by a mosquito. A big one. Then things get dangerous.

But it isn't the dead man cocooned inside a huge mass of web that worries the Doctor. It isn't the swarming, mutated insects that make him nervous.

With the village cut off from the outside world, and the insects becoming more and more dangerous, the Doctor knows that unless he can decode the strange symbols engraved on an ancient stone circle, and unravel a mystery dating back to the Second World War, no one is safe.

An original novel featuring the Twelfth Doctor and Clara, as played by Peter Capaldi and Jenna Coleman